Van Hillard lives and works in Washington, DC

Cover artwork designed by Cindy Biantoro Sharif – diamondhurts.blogspot.com

Future to the Back is a Dr. Clock production - copyright 2017

FUTURE TO THE BACK

Part 1: Certain Stars

Part 2: Uncertain Stars

Part 1: Certain Stars

"What is terrible in life goes on somewhere behind the scenes…"

— Dexter Chimney, Secretary of the Tragically Independent Department of Investigatory Services for Ectonormal Activities in the USA

~1~

Panic Attack from the Static in the Attic

On the tenth of November, 1982, Leonid Brezhnev, captain of an empire with eleven time zones, died in his sleep. This goofy slice of trivia gained its charisma with me because I had been reading a book about Brezhnev and his tenure of the Soviet Union on the day that my life capsized—on a tenth of November that fell about a nickel into the twenty-first century. Those spacious hours spent with Brezhnev and perpetual coffee would be the entrails of all of my previous years, those languid clones of tidy bohemia, and the beginning of something winged and fierce and wholly unfamiliar… That weird critter known in some social circles as *my future* was about to get spookier than a cold fart, because the convoy of events that were aroused on my tenth of November would lead me to declare the absurd: *I abolish death!*—my own death, at least—*and unlike Leonid Brezhnev I will not die in my sleep or any other fashion!*

(I hear you lathering your incredulity, but I tell you in the time and place I'm writing this from, you seldom see syllables like *lap* and *top* propped up next to each other.)

Brezhnev has since become a kind of code word in my life. When I question my alleged immortality, I think of Brezhnev lying there in his pajamas, stiller than an ancient ocean.

It all began with the panic attack in my attic—induced, no doubt, by autonomous static. I had gone up into my attic to do some thinking. There was nothing in particular needling my noodle, I had simply gone up there to *think* for a little while. Thinking was a favorite activity of mine, and the colorless confines of my attic sufficed aplenty for sincere thought arousal.

Once a month or so I'd climb up and perch myself cross-legged at my attic's tiny triangular window. Hours and hours I'd sit and reflect on all the things that had worked their way through my senses and into that mysterious comrade known as my memory. This wasn't necessarily a form of meditation. This wasn't Zen. I wasn't on the prowl for clarity or for enlightenment. Maybe if I got lucky I might wring a little harmony out of the whole endeavor, but primarily it simply felt cozy to be alone and mired in the contents of my brain.

It wasn't always a feel-good story, though. Ample times I'd plop back down into my hallway and my day-to-day feeling more confused about the world and my place within that world than I did before those hours in the attic. My faith in routine stood fast, though, and there I was again peering down at the unkempt urbanity of northeast Washington, DC from the severe angles of my attic.

My attic lacked the fusty clutter and the minefields of asbestos that you'd usually associate with an attic. The house I lived in was recently remodeled and my attic was seldom trodden. It was a bare and unremarkable attic, if not spookily so. The only thing unusual about it at all was the metal hatch that I entered it through, the same metal hatch that failed to open for me upon my desired departure—that is, when I saw the static.

My attic was haunted, but it wasn't haunted with ghosts. My attic was haunted with static.

Where did the static come from? And why was it in my attic? And why my *attic* and not my living room? Or my study? Or my equally spooky cellar? This is the trim breed of question that stampeded around my brain when I encountered the static, questions that, for better or worse, have largely been quashed by equally wayward answers.

I was sitting at the window, my eyes glazed in lost thoughts. I say "lost" but I remember exactly where my thoughts had wandered off to. They'd wandered off to the usual place—that is, they'd wandered off to *women.* I'd only just been thinking of something progressively serious, far removed from the bowels of my id, but three sly segues was all it took, and there I was thinking about women again. Specifically I was thinking about some Lori or Lora from yesteryear who spoke with her hands, or rather, everything she said with her mouth she would enunciate with her hands, and the years of doing so had turned an otherwise simple conversation with her into a thoroughly entertaining piece of performance art: a routine that I continually refrained from pointing out in worry that an introduction to any level of self-awareness might hinder her performance and possibly even persuade her to lose the gesticulation bit completely and just speak with her mouth like everyone else.

Still sitting at the window in my attic, I began to undress the girl in my head. I had an ambitious libido and it took little incentive for it to assert itself. The girl was shedding layers with jujitsu swiftness. One by one by one they came off, as she sat cross-legged up against the wall of my mind's eye… *Adios, cashmere sweater. Adios, bra. See ya later, stockings. Nice knowing ya, thong thingy…* Zero clothes. Eden or bust. I got hung up on a little horizontal crevice on the girl's stomach that occurred when she leaned up, a fault line of sorts in her minimalist pudge. She leaned back and it disappeared, a pink afterimage took its place. My attention swerved elsewhere. Other senses rabidly introduce themselves to the situation…. I closed my eyes and they stayed that way for a while, intoxicated by sloth and dull lust. Real sad day for the however many deadly sins we were up to… Wake me when the fat lady starts wrangling with the mic stand…

I opened my eyes and about five feet in front of me was some strange airborne phenomenon, vaguely rectangular in shape but so thin and flimsy that I could hardly make out its edges. I stared at it for a while, eyes glazed in bewilderment. Its presence grew stronger and stronger. Suddenly, I realized exactly what I was looking at…

Static.

Television static.

At first I felt a queer nostalgia. I hadn't seen television static in, what, ten years? *Twenty* years? Not since way back when TV didn't yet cater to insomniac audiences, and instead offed itself at a slender hour each night in a fierce swirl of depleted hues.

Static. Technology's Hungry Ghost, with its radiant hiss and manic flux. Implied faces drifting and falling and nibbling at each other. Pixilated bedlam. Ecto-humanity and zero fun.

It was a rude reintroduction to this thing called static. I continued to stare at the static, loosely wondering what business it had doing in my attic. It hovered in the same three dimensions as me, and its edges pushed and pulled in conflicting directions. The static, it seemed, was becoming increasingly erratic. The evening sunlight barely illuminated the attic. I stared at the static until my eyes began to burn. Then I blinked a lot and rubbed my eyes.

I devised a plan of action:

Scram!

I jumped up and ran to the hatch, which was impossibly yet undoubtedly *locked*. I tugged hard on the hatch to no avail. In the meantime, the static had abandoned its rectangular shape and taken on one of amoebic dimensions. And through my own frantic glossolalia of clipped curse words, I could hear a menacing hiss that grew louder as the static wavered its way closer. My skin glowed and tingled with the throbbing tug of electricity. Every hair on my body stood on end, like I was encircled by a thousand encroaching televisions.

And then the static spoke:

"I wouldn't do that if I were you."

Its voice was androgynous and synthetic. It was like a collective of the universal media channeled by every television ever, each word composed of a dozen timbres from voices out of the past, present, and future. It was the sound of residual humanity filtered through its technological extensions and spat back out as some weird, amorphous gobbet, sapped of all emotion, dry of everything that was ever human about it.

I stopped tugging on the hatch. I had worn myself out in a frenzied state of panic and I was certain my bones and muscles would tell me all about it at a later time. I stood up and squared myself at the static, which now hovered at navel's height six or seven feet away.

"You wouldn't do what if you were me?"

"Yank on that hatch like that," the static said. It made a sound like it was clearing its throat, and then with a different voice—male, singular, and decidedly hokey—it said: "You'll screw up your back."

My fear waned and a husky dose of bafflement seeped in.

"Relax, friend. I come in peace," the static said. "And a word of advice: Don't spend so much time thinking dirty stuff."

"Dirty stuff?" I countered, equal parts vertebrae and caution. "I definitely was not thinking dirty stuff."

"Yeah? Then what's that gal doing up there on the tiptop of your brain unpeeling herself?" said the static. "Lies and me ain't exactly chocolate and peanut butter, friend. I suggest you ease up with the fibbin' business." The static then see-sawed its way toward the ceiling, stopping only inches away. Its shape had returned to its original rectangular form but its glow had grown consistently brighter.

"What the hell *are* you?" I asked.

"Well, for starters, I'm omniscient," said the static.

Again I asked the static what it was and it seemed to wince and briefly wavered like a flag in the wind. It stilled itself and said, "Prepare to be surprised."

"I'm already sufficiently surprised."

"What I'm about to tell you is even more, uh, surprising."

I said nothing.

"I'm God," said the static.

"No way."

"*Yes* way," the static said. "I'm God alright. And unless you dig the idea of sitting around and watching your flesh sizzle for an eternity 'n a half, I recommend you take my word for it." The static's pixilated madness cooperated long enough to form an image of Christ on the cross and then returned to its natural state of flux.

"You're *the* God?"

"What other god you want me to be? Yes, I'm *the* God—or Jehovah, Yahweh, whatever name you want to use. All the same to me."

"That's fucking crazy, man."

"Whoa, watch your mouth, chief."

The static briefly formed a wagging finger. I got a little indignant.

"How about a little proof, God."

"Yeah, okay, *Thomas*." Touché.

The static curled inward like the pouch of a sling-shot. Was it taking a deep breath? "Your name is Everett Carmel Doyle. Everett comes from the German surname *Eberhard*, which roughly translates to 'brave boar'—"

"Brave boar?"

"—which is derived from the German *eber* or 'wild boar' and *hard* which means 'brave' or 'hardy'. You were given the middle name Carmel because you were conceived in a hotel in Carmel, California, population 1,084 circa 1974. The hotel you were conceived in was part of a now long-defunct chain of hotels called Conception Inn. You might've heard of Carmel because actor/director Clint

Eastwood was actually mayor there from 1986 to 1988. Your last name, Doyle, is...."

"Okay, okay, you're God."

"Far out, eh?"

"Yeah, real mind-blowing," I said. "You know, I could've lived a thousand years without knowing I was conceived in a Conception Inn."

"But you believe me now, eh?"

"Sure I do, at least more than I did ten seconds ago," I said. "What's with this static get-up though?"

The top two tips of the static extended down and tugged at the bottom two tips, like it was checking itself out. "This is actually my natural state. My birthday suit, as it were," the static said. "Ever read a book by the name of Genesis?"

"Yeah, I read Genesis, but that was like thirty years ago," I said. "I read it in Sunday school. I thought we looked like you, though. I thought we were designed in your image."

"Yeah, a lot of things didn't translate very well. It's an old book, you know. Tough back then to getting a hold of a decent translator, nevermind an editor worth his loincloth. Put a water pistol to their head and they still can't spell Deuteronomy."

"Why not revise it?" I said, "Or flex your omnipotence and just change the whole thing?"

"I'd love to, but it's not so easy changing something that people have grown so comfortable with. What if Francis Ford Coppola just *decided* to change the ending of the Godfather? What if Sonny had lived and became the Don instead of Michael? Or even something minor like if Michael had let Carlo live. It would be anarchy."

"True, true." He was right. Had Michael let Carlo live, it would have been a completely different movie.

The static, or God, began to wobble and fall from the ceiling as its glow grew dimmer and thinner.

"You're probably wondering why the heck I'm up here in your attic."

"That's definitely on the list of things I'm wondering about, yeah," I said.

"It's not often I intervene like this—in my birthday suit on a Wednesday afternoon in someone's attic. It's quite rude of me, I know. I may be known to many people for many things, but rudeness isn't ordinarily one of them."

I thought about this. It *was* rather rude of Him to materialize in my attic, especially during one of my thinking sessions. I recalled how terrified I was only moments ago—no difficult task considering my heart was still galloping audibly.

"Understand, though, that I'd never be so obtrusive if the matter at hand weren't of such high priority," the static, or God, said as it formed a brief exclamation point. "Everett, I have an urgent favor to ask of you."

"Just name it. I owe you plenty for all that heathenism in my twenties. You remember what I said about you after reading Krishnamurti and Alan Watts?"

"Of course I remember. I don't hold it against you, though. You were young and naïve. Tons and tons of youngsters blaspheme me every single day on the calendar. They get a hold of a little Nietzsche and you'd think I'd keyed their Mazda."

"I don't doubt it," I said. "So what's the favor?"

"On December 16th of…what year is this?"

"What do you mean *what year is this?*"

"It's two thousand something, right?" God said. "C'mon, just tell me."

I told Him what year it was.

"Look, I may be omniscient and omnipotent, but I'm also *eternal*, so asking me what year it is is like asking you what second it is. Do you know what second it is?"

"No, of course I don't."

"I didn't think so. Look, I'm sorry. I just get so dang burnt out of having to prove myself all the time."

God's voice sounded increasingly familiar. It fluctuated between the truculent nasal growl of Edward G. Robinson and the hokey murmur of Jimmy Stewart. Altogether, God was beginning to weird me out.

"Anyway, December 16th. Pretty sure it's a Monday. I need you to go to the Convention Center at 10am. Go to room 14. There will be a bunch of people sitting around. Join them and tell them you're here for the contest."

"The contest?"

"Yes, the contest for the next voice of the Washington Metrorail."

"The voice of the Metro?"

"Yeah, the voice *on* the Metro. You know, the voice that says *Step back, doors closing!*" God said, perfectly duplicating the current Metro voice.

"You want me to actually audition?"

"Correct."

"You think I got a shot at winning?"

"You *do* win. You win the thing unanimously."

"No kidding?"

"No kidding."

I pondered this for a second and tried to imagine how my voice would sound as the Metro voice. "How the hell do I win?"

"Well, you have a very pleasant voice," God said. "And that's what they're looking for, a very pleasant voice."

I had indeed been told before that I had a pleasant voice, but I would have never in a thousand years considered it to competitively pleasant.

"Sure, my voice is pleasant, but it ain't that pleasant," I said.

"Well, it doesn't really matter how pleasant it is or ain't because I already took care of it."

"Took care of it?"

"Yeah, you know, *took care* of it."

"You rigged the contest?"

"Yes, sir."

Neat stuff, getting to be the voice of the Metro, corruptly or otherwise. I nodded in accord while loosely thinking about the possibilities of all this.

"You are okay with all this?" God said, with a humdrum that sounded maybe a little blistered with impatience.

"I'm totally okay with all this," I said. "Sounds like a neat experience." Neat experiences and I would be boof buddies before it was all said and done.

"Well, I can't thank you enough, Everett," God said. "But what I can do is a little financial favor for you. Got a pen?"

I frisked my pockets already knowing damn well I didn't have a pen and shrugged.

"Commit this to memory." His pixels formed a series of hyphenated numbers: 42-66-68. "That's Friday's winning numbers in the Triple Whammy. The pot's up to like $36,000. Not a ton of money, but for you it is."

"Goddamn right. Decent little chunk of dough as far as I'm concerned. Shit. Sorry, man," I said, awash in sincere guilt. "I didn't mean to say 'GD'…"

"Don't sweat it."

God and I shared an awkward silence.

"Well, I should probably skedaddle," God offered lazily. "Super duper busy as you can probably imagine. And I have to be on Akfakznarf by sundown their time."

"What the heck is that?"

"Akfakznarf? It's this dumb planet way the heck out in Andromeda. Very similar to Earth, only the highest form of evolution there are these huge beetle-like insects."

"Evolution?"

"Yeah, evolution. My finest creation yet."

"Oh, God..."

"What?"

"Nothing, nothing," I said. "Hey, it's been an immense pleasure."

"Likewise!"

"December 16th, 10am, Convention Center, room 14, audition."

"Perfecto. Also, don't drink coffee or anything else with caffeine in it before the audition. And no cigarettes or booze the night before."

"Understood."

"Take care, friend." The pixels formed a waving hand.

"You do the same," I said, waving back.

Wowsers. I opened the hatch (with ease now) and steadied myself on the ladder. Something popped into my head and I said to God, "Hey, before you split, can I ask you something?"

"Sure, go for it."

I contemplated my question for a second and then said, "Does a person actually have a soul?"

God had shrunk to the size of a Gameboy. "Yes. People have souls. Every single person is born with a soul."

"Wild," I said, contemplating this. "That's real wild. Where's it located?"

"You really wanna know?'

"Absolutely, I really wanna know."

God's pixels formed a person's face. The face opened its mouth very wide and the screen zoomed in on a perfectly formed pair of tonsils.

"Tonsils, eh?"

"Yes, sir."

Crud. Heavy news, that. Oh well. I said bye again and climbed down the ladder and plopped down at my dining table. I replayed the whole exchange in my head. Eventually my belly starting growling so I went into the kitchen where I made myself a peanut butter and banana sandwich and said grace for maybe the first time in fifteen years.

~2~

The Passes Break the News

"Words…," said the man on TV whose house was flattened by a tornado, "Words… jus' can't describe what I'm feeling. They jus'…can't describe it."

Sure, they can. How about: *I feel speechless.*

The man's house and dozens more were leveled last night when a tornado swept through some anonymous county in central Virginia. The man, his wife, and their three children had hid in the bathtub with a mattress on top of them. Their frequently mentioned dog, Riley, was presumed dead.

"They jus' can't describe it…"

How about: *I feel like I'm in a state of shock because I'm coming to terms with being homeless.*

The man's wife wore a permanent worried expression. No doubt from accumulating a lifetime's worth of *temporary* worried expressions. Misfortune personified, still among the living because of a bathtub and a mattress. In her hand she held a plastic zip-lock bag with a goldfish in it.

"Words jus' can't…they can't express it…"

How about: *I'm in a state of ineffable consternation.*

"No words…no words can express…"

How about: *I'm goddamned pissed as fuck.*

I turned off the TV and went upstairs to ready myself for the competition. As promised, my Triple Whammy numbers came up and I was now $36,000 wealthier (decidedly less after taxes). I abstained from booze and cigarettes, no difficulty as a newborn teetotaler/non-smoker. I guzzled orange juice and had some Cozy Chamomile with lemon and honey.

I'd just applied a fingerful of pomade to my hair when the phone rang. God, maybe? Or perhaps a friendly reminder by way of one of his angels. Maybe even Gabriel or Michael.

"Hello?"

"*Someone knockin' at the door, somebody ringin' a bell,*" sang a woman on the other end. She sounded muffled, like her phone was nestled between her head and shoulder.

"Hell*ooo?*"

"*...someone knockin' at...* Hello? Everett?"

"Yes, this is Everett," I said. "Who is this?"

"Let me in. I've been knocking on your door for like ten minutes. Are you in the bathroom?"

"Yes. I mean no. I'm fixing my hair. Who are you?"

"Just let me in, pretty please."

"Sure, sure, coming, coming." I washed my hands and shimmied down the stairs and opened the door.

"Hi, guy."

She had a postmodern pallor. Totally bleached out like a B-Movie vamp. Transparent, fading. Her eyes were all pupil, no iris, vacuous, and nestled underneath a set of eyebrows with sharp geometry—the eyebrows of caricatured statesmen and Hollywood Egyptians. Her lips were an exaggerated plush and artificially red, her nose was long and of suspicious symmetry. She had blue-black hair of indeterminate length pulled tightly into a little ball on the back of her head. She was without a widow's peak, an absence that kept her contrast in equilibrium. Puzzler of an age: either a mature twenty-something or a well-preserved thirty-something. She was wearing a flimsy black dress over a pair of shiny grey pants. She did not look friendly.

"Can I help you?"

"I certainly hope so," she said. "Though I admit I'm a wee skeptical."

It was early and I had not yet summoned up any cool to lose. "How do you know my name and my phone number?"

The girl funnied her face and said, "You're exceedingly trigger-happy with your personal information. Your personal bullshit is splattered all over the internet. Hell, I'd have to go out of my way *not* to know your name and number." She squinted into the midday sky and then frowned at me. "Jesus. All this daylight is destroying me. I can hear my epidermis whimpering. Any chance we can go inside?"

"I haven't decided if I want to let you in or not."

"Ah, gotcha. Let me know if you need any advice," she said with a tone that lacked sarcasm or malice. Standing there on the doorstep she made my synapses summon H.P. Lovecraft's *The Thing on the Doorstep*. The thing on the doorstep in *The Thing on the Doorstep* did not disappoint. Fortunately this girl was a different thing on a different doorstep. No way in this world or any other would the benignly sociopathic Howard Phillips Lovecraft let this peculiar critter in his house—one of many blaring differences between me and Mr. Lovecraft...

I stepped aside and motioned for her to come in. She walked in and immediately grimaced at the mid-size phalanx of maxed-out garbage bags that lurked near the entrance. We went into my living room. She had a backpack, although it wasn't on her back. She was carrying it with cautious surety as if it were a grocery bag full of eggs and light bulbs.

"Do you have somewhere safe I can put this?"

"Any flat surface should do."

"Right," she said. "You got any pets runnin' around?"

"Nope. I'm petless."

She set the backpack down and then commandeered several throw pillows from the adjacent couch and used them to form a little wall around it. I took a seat at my dining room table.

"What happened to your cat?" she asked from the living room.

"The little asshole dipped on me," I said. "Wait, how'd you know I had a cat?"

"Internet again," she said. "He's all over your stupid SpaceFace profile." She sat down next to the little wall of pillows. "What was his name? Mr. Scruff?"

"Yeah, Mr. Scruff," I said, getting a little annoyed at her bravado. "You're a regular Auguste Dupin, eh?"

She ignored the Dupin business and said, "Why'd you name him Mr. Scruff?"

"Because he was scruffy male cat. Is that satisfactory?"

"No, that is not at all satisfactory. That is the opposite of satisfactory," she said. "Naming a scruffy cat 'Mr. Scruff' denotes an immense dearth of creativity."

That wound me up even more. "You have no basis," I told her. "It took me weeks to come up with that name. I have a very thorough process for naming cats, roundabout but thorough, and I don't expect you, whoever you are, to understand the complexities of my cat-naming process."

"Relax, guy," she said, with this obnoxiously self-aware coziness. "You can name your next cat Maple McLeafy for all I care."

"—Question: Why are you here? I need to jet sooner than later, and...."

"It's bullshit," she said.

"What's bullshit?"

"Nobody needs a new voice for the Metro. It's bullshit."

She abruptly stood up and scooted across the imaginary line that separated my living room from my dining room and sat down next to across from me at the dining table.

"Don't bother trekking down to the Convention Center because there isn't any competition to be the voice of the Metro. That was bullshit. So you're not in any hurry. Lose your Keds and brew some coffee. Here's the scoop: I work for the *real* God and not the phony that paid you a visit the other day. If you go down to the Convention Center you'll be dead before *Wheel of Fortune* comes on."

I soaked up all this weird new info from this equally weird gal.

"My name is Mary Pass. I'm here because I need your assistance with an immensely distinct task. I would have come a hell of a lot sooner but I was locked up. The Devil—that's right, there's a fucking Devil—had me arrested in the Sudan. He paid off a bunch of dusty Taliban wannabees in Khartoum and they stuck me in a four-by-six cell for carrying one too many types of herbal shampoo," she said. "I'm sure you're more concerned about where you fit in to all this. My brother Tether Pass will provide you with 100% of the details. You actually met Tether years and years and years ago."

"Tether?" I chimed in. "I don't recall a Tether. I'd remember a Tether."

"You were at a pool party when you were seven years old. You were eating a plateful of BBQ ribs with the grace of a fucking werewolf and one of them got lodged in your throat. Tether saw you gagging so he gave you the Heimlich."

"I'll be damned," I said. "That dude was your brother? Super vague memory. I never knew his name or anything else about him. I only remember him telling me to learn how to chew. Actually he told me to learn how to *fucking* chew but I left that part out for my parents. What was he doing at that pool party?"

"Recon, my man," Mary said. "He was doing recon."

"Recon for what?"

She waved me off. "Just shush for a little minute, okay? One thing at a time. First, it is imperative that you go meet Tether today." She pulled what looked like a little paper airplane out of her pants pocket. "This contains your instructions. It's got all the who and the what and the where and the how and the when."

"What about the why?"

"The why is your destination, guy. Follow these instructions carefully and they'll lead you right to the why. X marks the why."

I took the little paper airplane. It was the snub-nose variety, good for flight-time but not distance. Long-hand cursive adorned the entirety of it.

"May I please use your restroom?" Mary asked.

"Go for it. It's— "

"—I'll find it."

She stalked upstairs in the direction of the restroom. I tip-toed over to her backpack and inspected it without touching it. Either my eyes were playing tricks on me or the backpack was gently moving. I inched closer, leaning in over the couch. No doubt about it, there was a definite movement about it; a slight and irregular pulsing as if hidden inside was some sleepy little animal.

"Don't touch that," Mary said from the top of the stairs. Startled, I jumped back and sheepishly returned to my seat like a chided schoolboy.

"What's in there?"

"Wingless honeybees."

I leaned up and peered at the backpack. "Really?"

"No, not really."

She descended the stairs, self-consciously pulling her dress down a bit even though she was wearing pants underneath it.

"It's a souvenir," she said. "A souvenir from Barcelona."

"Barcelona? I didn't think the Red Line went out that far."

My joke zoomed right through her and she said: "It's a weird wild world, Mr. Everett."

Indeed it is. And weirder and wilder every day apparently. I scratched my head and began to wonder if I was scratching it because I was perplexed or because other people, real and fictional, always seemed to scratch their heads when they were perplexed. In the end, I decided I was scratching my head because it actually itched.

"By the way, your toilet paper sucks," Mary said. "There are precisely two things you should never buy the leading brand of: Garbage bags and toilet paper." She glanced at an invisible watch on her wrist. "I gotta dangle. Until next time, mister…And again, please follow those instructions carefully." She put all the pillows back in their proper places and picked up her backpack.

I skimmed over my instructions. They were simple enough but there was no information about this Tether Pass at all, and the meta-memories of that day at the pool had long been rendered hazy. I only remembered him as, well, a *grown-up*.

"Hey, Mary," I called out as she was leaving. "How will I recognize your brother?"

She paused in the doorway and said, "He's the 974 year old."

I was to meet Tether Pass on the Metro at the Shaw-Howard station. He would be on the second car of the Greenbelt bound train at exactly 3:36 pm. I was assured there would be no delays on the Green Line.

I jumped aboard and looked around the car. Several intensely multicultural teens in college sweats were lumped together in a group. All smiles and yesteryear's slang. They were passing a digital camera around and taking pictures of each other. Various men and women hung from the poles, all of their noses embedded in some form of text. Only one of them was not reading, a man, though not particularly old looking, wearing a navy rain slicker and a black captain's hat complete with a little gold anchor. I would've put his age somewhere in his mid-fifties rather than 974. I raised a casual eyebrow at him and he mouthed the words *next stop*.

We exited the car and he motioned for me to follow him up one of the broken escalators. He shot up it in double-stride and I did a less than convincing job of mimicking him.

"Let's not talk until we get to where we need to be."

"Okay," I said. "Where exactly are we going?"

"Paolo's Pucker Palace. You know it? Doesn't matter. We're being followed so move quick."

"Being followed? Who's following us?"

No answer. We emerged from the subway and onto the barren stretch of yesteryear that was the northeast fringe of Shaw, or the caboose of the U Street Corridor. The sky was a gray swirl and the wind was strong enough to make us walk funny. The street we were on was once Shaw's main artery. I'd seen many a black and white photo displaying a neon swath of bustle and exchange, however, these days it was more akin to mid-'90s Groznyy. The street was lined with non-descript buildings, most of their entrances covered with aluminum sheeting or dark wooden planks, the sidewalk in front of them cluttered with garbage of brands that longer existed. A shoe repair place and a couple of dilapidated bus stops offered the only signs of civilization.

Tether Pass led me into the shoe repair place which further inspection revealed was also some sort of bar. It boasted an odd combo-smell of shoe polish and cigarette smoke, and its décor was a pish-posh of black and brown shoes and boots heaped along the wall and peering out of old oil drums. There were several framed pictures scattered about the wall, all of them of either mid-century DC or of shoes—exaggerated looking shoes with hilly curvature and so clean you could see the photographer's flash reflected on them. Several flannelled older men were husked together at the curve of the bar. Their flatline gray eyes took long but uncaring notice of our entry. At the opposite end sat a very ectomorphic black man, splayed and smiley, limbs everywhere. He was wearing a trim purple vest and a pair of sunglasses big enough to be mistaken for infra-red goggles. His matching purple fedora hung from his barstool like a catfish on a stringer. Sitting next to him was a short man with a red face and a short gray mustache snookered between a pair of bulldog cheeks. He was wearing a little gray communist cap and had a huge camera around his neck, and when I say huge I mean *huge*; the thing was oversized, double-wide, maybe a little bigger than the man's head and it had a lens with the circumference of a grapefruit. An elephant gun, only a *camera* instead of a gun.

"You been here before? Don't talk to nobody but me and my friends," said Tether. We plopped down in a booth big enough for a pair of hippos. The glossy purple seating reminded me of the bumper cars at a state fair.

"Shoes and booze, huh?"

"What? Listen, how'd you know it was me back there in the train? You spotted me pretty quick," said Tether.

"I don't know, I just knew."

"Bullshit." He must've picked this word up from his sister or vice versa.

"Well, there were a couple of little things," I said. "First, when the train took off, everyone that was standing up had to struggle a bit to keep a hold of their footing. Everyone but you. You were standing with your feet even with your shoulder blades and when everyone else spazzed you just bent your knees slightly to lower your center of gravity, which I take it you know is located at your navel. I figured if anybody knew where their center of gravity is it's the 974 year old."

"I learned that when I was six."

"Also, you weren't reading anything. Why the hell would a 974 year old want to read something when he's got his memory?"

"That's good, but I left my book at the hotel. A pirate book. I knew some of 'em. This guy wrote the book's got 'em all wrong. Cook was a sissyboy. Straight up sissyboy."

I loosed a nervous little laugh and took a look around Paolo's. I'd been to places like this before, though not quite like this. The city's crustier no-go zones were dotted with rickety bars with forgotten beers on draft and many of these bars were now trafficked by weekend booze buds who'd splurge on cab fare so they could spend half a buck less on their beer and revel in temporary squalor and the illusion of being broke and broken. When the final last call arrived they would spill into the street with mock abandon until the crouching silhouettes of the natives spurred them to slink over to their waiting cabs. Many of these dives over the years began to embrace their dive-dom, slacking on repairs, intentionally downsizing their jukeboxes rather than upgrading them, refraining from dusting and mopping and emptying their garbage cans. A contemptible set of affairs, that scene. Though, this place, I could tell, was different from all that. This place you wouldn't come across in the least lustrous travel guide.

"Drink?" Tether asked me.

"I'm good, thanks."

"Nothin'?"

"Maybe a ginger ale."

"You don't drink?"

"Nah, I gave it up. You don't get teeth like this from eating too many oatmeal cookies," I said, showing him the miniature South Bronx inside my mouth.

"C'mon, one skinny little beer ain't gonna muss your mane."

I resigned to his request. After all, a beer would probably help quash the spiky little caterpillar that was doing somersaults on my nervous system.

Paolo turned out to be the little red-faced man with the giant camera. He patted his companion on the hand and scampered around the bar to fetch our beers; then he waltzed over to us with the beers held up high like a pair of prize fish. He pulled up a small stool that looked like a birdbath and sat down.

"Didn't see you sneak in," he said to Tether. Then he extended his hand to me and said, "Paolo. Pleasure to me you, sir."

"Everett. Likewise."

"So this is our man," he said to Tether.

"Allegedly."

Paolo looked me up and down with a frozen smile on his face that in a different context would've passed for a smile of supreme lechery. He held up his hands like he wanted to play patty-cake. "Hey, Deanwood," he yelled to the man at the bar. The man snagged his hat and strutted over with a ten inch grin.

"Deanwood, this is Everett Doyle, our new playpal," Tether said.

"What's shakin', Halloween?"

It took me a long five seconds to realize the man was referring to my ill choice of color coordination: a bright orange v-neck sweater over a black undershirt. He extended one of those long arms of his and we shook hands.

"Mr. Tether here told us all about you." He took off his shades/goggles and pulled up a seat. He was sodden with Drakkar Noir. "He says you the nicest dude in the whole wide world. You really that nice?"

"What do you mean?"

"I mean are you really as nice as Mr. Tether says you are?"

"Let up with it, Deanwood," Tether said. "He don't even know why he's here yet."

The jukebox physically lurched forward and loudly popped several times before emitting some muffled tango music. I immediately recognized it as my second favorite Argentinean (the #1 slot still occupied by Jorge Luis Borges).

"This is Astor Piazzola," I said, staring up at nothing, ear cocked.

"It is indeed Astor Piazzola," said Paolo. "I'm very impressed that you recognize him. Are you a fan?"

"I am a fan. I've dug him for years and years. This is the first track off of the cynical dancer and the…"

"*Rough Dancer and the Cyclical Night*," Paolo said. "It is a very enchanting collection. Actually it is one of my favorite works of all time—and that's a bold statement coming from a self-proclaimed tango snob."

"Yeah, it's a pretty neat album, for damn sure," I said. "It's also immensely elusive. I don't think I've ever heard outside of my headphones…Accolades aplenty, sir, for having it on your jukebox."

"Thank you," Paolo said. "It is always a pleasure to encounter another Piazzola enthusiast."

"You know what I call this shit?" said Deanwood. "Commie music."

"That's because you have no culture," Paolo shot back.

"This is the shit they listen to in countries with flags that got Kalashnikovs and palm trees on 'em," Deanwood said, lightly grabbing my wrist for emphasis. "Countries where they don't play soccer in the soccer stadiums, if you know what I mean."

I knew what he meant.

"Enough about the fucking music," said Tether.

There was no way for me to know at the time, but the Piazzola track off *Rough Dancer and the Cyclical Night* that we were listening to, lazily titled Prologue, was the unofficial leitmotif of Tether Pass and his peculiar posse. I wouldn't hear it again until a distant Denver night way on down the line, when one Pal Iberville, Tether's hired set of dukes, would step out of the shadows and lay into my torso like he was getting paid fifteen bucks an hour plus tips to do so…

Tether Pass took turns staring at me and Paolo and Deanwood and finally said: "Everett, we need your help. The four of us—me, these two music lovers, and my sister Mary who you met earlier—need your help. We are what you might call ambassadors from God. Only it's not the God you think it is. That God don't exist. The God we came from is us. God as humanity, or vice versa. It was us the whole time, Everett. Except now we know it. We know it because that's where we're from. We get there, alright. Man, woman, whatever, we get there. It takes a long damn time. Almost sixteen-hundred more years but we get there. We finally turn into the God that made us. A big dandy cycle: we're God, we're not God, we think we might be God, we think someone else is God, we think we're God again, we're certain we *have* to be God, then we *are* God, then it's the total thing so we start over again."

"The future, Halloween. We come from the future *and* the past, don't make no difference to us," said Deanwood.

I wrinkled my brow for probably the tenth time that day. "What do you guys need from me?"

"You're a nice guy, Everett. The nicest," said Tether.

"How many enemies you got, Halloween?"

I thought about this. I remember as recently as five years ago realizing that I didn't have a single known enemy in the world and I was afraid that not much had changed since.

"Zero," said Deanwood. "Wanna know *why* you ain't got no enemies? Real simple. You, sir, realize that everything in the world is always changin'. For example, I'm not even the exact same person I was when I came over and sat down. I've done lost about a million cells since I was over there at the bar. And I gained stuff, too. Bacteria, microbes… I've got volcanic ash in my hair that wasn't even *in this room* ten seconds ago. Now, say, a year ago? Why, we're talking a whole different person. Two years ago? Shit, I don't even recognize the guy. You telling me you want to hold a grudge on someone you don't know? Circumstances, Halloween. You realize—and not many people do—that it's all about circumstances. Events. That's what we all really are, Halloween. Events. How you gonna go get mad at an event? People always changin', every second. Even when they ain't changin', they changin'. Just events like everything else. Damn sure ain't as solid as we like to think we are. You get mad at some dude for some stupid shit, you might as well get mad at thunder for being so loud, or this damn music for being so, I don't know, fruity soundin'…Thing is, I'm telling you this, but I know you know it all already. I'm just remindin' you, is all. So when I'm saying you're a nice guy, what I mean is that you're one of us. You're a remarkable event that can reflect on itself. Except what we're takin' it further, Halloween. Those rules was made by us. And we can rewrite 'em. Any damn time we want, we can rewrite 'em."

I watched Deanwood's lips move but I'd given up on his theory about halfway through it. What kind of lousy world would we be living in if people were always letting each other off the hook? Besides, I wasn't nice. I'd never thought of myself as a nice person. I was just complacent. I was a milquetoast. There were plenty of people out there who I wouldn't mind seeing win a trip to Loose Tooth City but that didn't mean I was going to do anything about it. I didn't have any enemies because I simply wasn't equipped with the willpower it takes to maintain an enemy. The people I didn't like I simply avoided or treated indifferently.

"Your niceness is what's gonna bail us out. You know what a homunculus is?" asked Tether. He had yet to take a sip of his beer.

A homunculus? Had I heard him right? "A homunculus is the little person that supposedly lives inside of you operating you. It's Latin for 'little man'," I said to them.

"Check it out, our boy knows Latin… And you're right, that's exactly what a homunculus is. As it is, we got a very special homunculus and he needs a home real quick-like. Problem is he's got expensive taste. Won't settle for just any old home. He wants the richest man in the world for a home."

"The richest man in the world?" I asked.

"*The* richest man in the world."

"Houston, Halloween," said Deanwood.

"Houston?"

"Dallas Austin Houston," said Tether.

"The richest man in the world."

"Yes, Dallas Austin Houston, the richest goddamned son-of-a-bitch on this planet or any other," said Deanwood.

"The oil guy? The Texan?"

"Yeah, the Texas oil guy," said Tether.

"Actually, he was born in England," said Deanwood. "Somethin'-shire."

"*Devon*shire," said Paolo.

"But now he's a Texan," said Tether.

"How you like Texas, Halloween?"

"How do I like Texas? I don't like Texas. Cruddy landscape. Lackluster cities that sprawl forever. And a lot of the people that live there think their state is superior just because it's geographically bigger than all the other states."

"The other *contiguous* states," said Paolo.

"Well, yeah, that's what I mean."

"Man, our boy definitely doesn't like Texas," said Deanwood. "That's ok, though, because where he's goin' is actually *underneath* Texas."

I looked at the three of them looking at me. Clarity spoke up and I momentarily realized what an abnormal situation I was in. What would Leonid Brezhnev think about all this? Who the heck knows, man.

"Heavy shit, no doubt about it, Halloween. Just hang in there."

Tether said to me, "We need you to go into Houston's bunker. Leave him with the homunculus while he's sleeping."

"Houston's bunker?"

"Yeah, he's got a bunker. It's like his home base or his headquarters or whatever. Houston's *Houston*, so to speak. It's about a half-mile beneath the dirt just next to a little Mexican joint just outside San Antonio. A little Mexican joint that looks a wee better nourished than the other ones around it."

"You want me to go to this Houston guy's bunker and give him a homunculus."

"Well, you're not going to give it to him. You're going to leave it with him while he's sleeping."

"Sure, sure, why not," I said, flippantly. "You know what, gentlemen? This whole thing's goofy. You guys are goofy."

"We're not goofy," said Tether. "We can get goofy, though. You want us to get goofy?"

I didn't want them to get goofy. I decided to lay off the lip.

"You're going to get a job at Houston's bunker. Head of Security. The only thing friendlier than your face is your resume," said Tether.

"I don't have a resume. I've never had a resume in my life," I said.

"Deanwood, show goofy guy his resume."

Deanwood pulled out a folded up piece of paper from his back pocket and handed it to me. I read it up and down a couple of times, while the three of them got some muffled kicks from watching my reaction.

"This is heavy duty. I was a pilot?"

"Yep. Ex-military. Very necessary. And you don't pass for a grunt," said Tether.

"NASA security?"

"Somebody's gotta watch them rockets while they sleep."

"University of Texas football program?"

"Your last name's too short for a kicker. So we made you the punter. What do you know about baseball?"

"I know plenty about baseball."

"Learn plenty more. Especially about shortstops. You tried out for the Portland Sea Dogs. Get to know your Ozzies."

"Did I make the team?"

"Negative. Jeep accident. Totaled your Wrangler. Other guy's fault. Broke both your pinkies."

"You've got to be kidding."

"Shit, we gotta work on his accent," said Deanwood to Tether. "Say *you gotta be kiddin'.*"

"You gotta be kiddin'."

"Say *nekked.* That's what you are when you got no clothes on, you're nekked."

"Nekked."

"And when you put on your clothes, you're not *about* to put on your clothes, you're *fixin'* to put on your clothes."

"I'm fixin' to put on my clothes," I mimicked. "What kind of plane did I fly?"

"A-10 Warthog. A tank killer," said Tether.

"But that's an Army plane. I wasn't in the Air Force?"

"Nope, Army. See, our boy already knows about planes. This is gonna be easy cheese."

"What was my handle?" I asked.

"Something Falcon," said Deanwood.

"*Red* Falcon," said Tether.

"Red Falcon? I don't know about Red Falcon. Kinda goofy."

"Everything's goofy to you, eh?"

A series of "holy shits" from the lumpy men at the bar led my attention to the little black and white television at the end of the bar. It was displaying a frenzy of some sort. A none-too-stable cameraman was filming dozens of policemen setting up camp outside of what I immediately noticed to be the Convention Center.

"Whoa, something's screwy downtown. Check it out..." I said while squinting at the TV.

"Everett. The thing in your attic the other day..." said Tether. "That was Kyle."

"*Kyle?*"

"Kyle is a trickster spirit."

"*The* trickster spirit, Halloween," said Deanwood.

"You may know him by his alias: Coyote," said Paolo breaking his silence and pulling him back from the Piazzola, "He is the sum of all abandoned technology, an orphaned bastard of humanity's extensions—and he has a vendetta."

"Who's he got a vendetta against?"

"Against *us*, Everett," Paolo replied, "Against humanity. He likes us where we are and isn't too keen about us making any sort of transcendental maneuvers. He's most comfortable when we're squirming. He delights in the misery of others and adores mischief. Only he lacks foresight. He lacks the ability to see that if humanity goes away he will no longer have anyone to sabotage."

"But what about this voice of the Metro business?"

"Kyle, as you might expect from a trickster spirit, is an excellent liar. Have you ever told a lie before, Everett? A good lie, a believable lie, has to have the proper level of abstraction or complexity in order for it to be convincing beyond a doubt. An example: for some dubious reason or another you're late to pick up your girlfriend from the airport. You need a reasonable excuse, or a reasonable *lie*. You wouldn't want to say you got stuck watching TV and lost track of time; you'd want to elaborate, turn it into an intriguing story. You'd want to tell her that you were just about to leave when you went downstairs and your roommate was watching a show on the History Channel about the Battle in the Aleutian Islands, which your grandfather had participated in as a tail-gunner in a B-24 Liberator. Come to find out your roommate's grandfather had *also* been involved in the Battle of the Aleutian Islands, had also been stationed at the Adak Island airbase and had been a *nose*-gunner on a B-24 Liberator. Next thing you know you were searching through your closet to find a picture of your grandfather's airplane and your roommate was on the phone calling his parents in Georgia to see if they had a picture of his grandfather's plane. An hour passes and suddenly you're late to pick up your girlfriend. Who wouldn't believe such a thing?"

"Kyle was fibbin' you," continued Tether. "Granted this fib had a little more basis in reality. Had you gone to room 14 in the convention center you'd be dead, along with everybody else there. Shot up by a schizoid with a deer rifle. Mass murder, friend."

"Whoa."

"You see, that's one bitter fellow up there," said Tether. "Beyond bitter. Furious. Looks like he finally got so wound up he went out his noodle. Forty-five years of being taunted by a singular sour memory, a real reeker from a school playground of long ago. The man doing all the shooting in there is Al Key, the current voice of the Metro. The '*step back, doors closing!*' guy. Kyle paid Al Key a visit right after he came to you in your attic. He pulled the same 'I'm God' bullshit on him and told him that the Metro people were looking for a new voice because they'd gotten many complaints about his voice being—get this—*too squirrelly*. This in itself should be pretty rotten news for Al, but it gets better—or worse, I should say. Al Key had a big time crush in third grade named Molly Boysenberry. This Boysenberry ended up messing Al up more than she'll ever know. Al was the quintessential shy guy, he left Boysenberry little presents in her desk: flowers he'd picked, plastic rings from gumball machines, he even got her a souvenir #2 pencil from her home state of Oregon. He would peek at her as she picked up and examined each of his gifts with the same sturdy empiricism and then nonchalantly place it back inside her desk as if it were just a trapper keeper or one of her text books. This spurred him to continue the gifts with more frequency. He went from one every month to one every week: a Plymouth Rock paper weight, a locust shell, cereal box toys, a Scooby Doo flashlight. He waited for one of them to be the transcendental gift that would make her peer over at him and stretch her lips and twinkle her eyes. But she didn't do that. What she did was tell her teacher to tell whoever's giving her gifts to cut it out. A lousy move from an arrogant little spoiled brat. But it wasn't Boysenberry's little blond pony tail that Al had fallen in love with, or the way she looked in her little plaid skirt. Al Key kept chasing her because he knew deep down that she was utterly unattainable. Not in a million years would she go out with him and he knew it. But the impossibility of it made his desire grow stronger and throughout his life it began to manifest in other arenas. Al Key has led a life of chasing unattainable goals: too short to be a fighter pilot, too asthmatic to be a scuba diver, too this, not enough that. Finally, one day he gets his moment of glory: He wins the voice of the Metro competition and passengers everywhere in the city follow his anonymous commands every day of the week. But Kyle brings Boysenberry back around to haunt him. *Your voice is too squirrelly so they're scrapping it*, he says to him. No big deal? Wrong. One day long ago on the playground Little Al Key caught Boysenberry playing a game of tether ball by herself…

"It was me that gave you all those gifts," he says.

"I kinda knew," she says.

"Did you like them?" he asks.

"Some of them," she says.

"Which ones?" he asks.

"I don't know. The ones that weren't spooky, I guess," she says.

"I can give you more if you want. I can give you expensive gifts" he says.

"Better not," she says.

"Would you like a ring? I could give you a real pretty ring. One that's not plastic," he says.

"No thanks," she says.

"What's your favorite color? Mine's turquoise," he says knowing already that hers is turquoise.

"Mine's red," she says.

"Do you want to be boyfriend and girlfriend?" he asks.

"Better not," she says.

"You're kinda squirrelly," she says.

"Plus I already have a boyfriend," she says.

"So what Kyle does," said Tether, "is makes it out to be a big conspiracy: *The people of Washington, D.C. deserve better than this squirrelly voice on their Metro system* kinda thing. What Al doesn't know, and thanks to about two dozen bullet holes in his body will never know, is that those people in room 14 aren't there for any subway voice competition. They're all members of the National Mensa Material Club. They're a bunch of geniuses that gather together once a month to drink bubbly in the afternoon and talk about how smart they are. Thing is, you can invent Kevlar but it don't do you much good if you ain't wearing it when you need to be. Al Key just mowed down about fifteen rocket scientists and he would've gotten you too had you listened to your boy up in the attic."

I sighed and let all this new info flop around in my noodle. Deanwood and Paolo had wandered over to the TV. From what I could tell, it had been confirmed that Al Key, or Albert Kenneth Key as he was already being referred to as, was indeed the shooter, had indeed blasted "several" members of the National Mensa Material Club, and had indeed been pumped full of SWAT team bullets. I would later learn what a fabulous sense of humor a trickster spirit is capable of possessing as the media would bring to light the fact that this Albert Kenneth Key had recently been swiftly denied a membership to the National Mensa Material Club because his test results had rendered him to be of "adequate" intelligence. *What does the world think of you, Mr. Key? A deluxe goober of adequate intelligence, Mr. Key, that's the sum of it. Go get 'em, Mr. Key. Don't forget to take the safety off...*

Tether sat twisted around in his seat and stared at the television. I examined his profile and for the first time realized what a flat face he had. Not unattractive, just extremely flat and shaped like a jouster's shield. His nose was a small job, not puggish and upturned, just smaller than the average nose while his mouth was that of a melancholy jack-o-lantern. His eyes were bright and alert with a touch of menace and had no notable baggage underneath them. His beard was as grey as his eyes and dense but cut very short.

He returned his attention to me. "You'll need to leave Thursday morning. That's three mornings from now. You're flying out of Baltimore. BWI. Quicker and cheaper, plus we got a badge on the payroll there that'll guarantee you and your little friend will make it through the gate. Mary can help you pack and do whatever else you got to do. Your job. You already quit, right? It was a shit job, anyway."

I had actually already turned in my notice at the *District Commuter*, my boss had known about my "lucky" run-in with the Triple-Whammy so there wouldn't be much mystery there.

"Deanwood will give you a copy of your resume as well as the dossier that Houston has on you. You'll need to brush up on both of them. Also get yourself a nice professional haircut and try doin' about a thousand push-ups before Thursday. Another thing: your clothes. Deanwood will help you out there, too. That foppish fuck knows all about that shit."

I finished my beer and had a moment of insight: What if this was all a prank? A very ridiculous and detailed prank of unknown origins? In the end I decided it was simply too bizarre to be false—and besides, who the hell would want to take the time to plan all of this out just to pull one over on me? Not to mention go about gathering this cast of personified question marks whose company I was currently in. My standards for the bizarre, however, were ultimately nothing short of tremendous and I recalled on more than one occasion boasting of life itself being so bizarre that any subcategory of it was inherently incapable of being more bizarre. This was an argument I routinely defended Christians and other faith-based groups with, even though I was not a Christian nor did I latch on to any particular other variety of faith (I had decided to save that whole bit for the deathbed). Altogether I found them to be no less benighted than the firm believers of science, those self-proclaimed destroyers of the relevance of religions of the world. I'd gathered that a very high number of them had never actually seen an electron and a very *very* high number had not actually seen an electron acting outside of observation. Once again, more faith. I did applaud their efforts, however, and I most certainly utilized their discoveries each and every day although I disregarded the arrogance of their chiefs and shamans.

"When was the last time you saw an electron?" I asked Tether.

"Two days ago. *Three* days ago. Saturday, whenever that was. Why?"

"Nevermind."

"One more thing. You're Badger now. Everett Carmel Badger. Doyle don't work. Too close to 'Pyle.' Bad connotations. Doesn't fit with the schematic, if you will."

"Badger?"

"That's right, Badger, like the varmint."

"Why Badger?"

"Why Badger, he says. Why *not* Badger? Why not Wolverine? Makes no difference. Too late to change it anyway. One more thing," this guy was full of *one more things.* "Who'd you vote for last election?"

"I didn't vote for anyone."

"Nobody?"

"Nope. Nobody. I'm deceivingly apolitical."

"Not anymore you're not. You voted. And you voted for Trant. The bubble-butt from Texas."

"Trant?"

"Yeah, Trant. *Deceivingly apolitical.* Where'd you get off with that? Lazy is what you mean. You're lazy."

"I have my reasons not to vote."

Within the span of a second, the hint of menace in Tether Pass's eyes spread outward devouring every feature of his face. "Every knucklehead on the planet has their reason for every silly piece of business they do or don't do. I'm only interested in what you do according to the dossier. You do understand that. And unless you got a thing for man-size nets and straightjackets and really austere decor, I recommend you keep your lips nice and zipped, you dig?"

I dug.

"Okay, boy," Tether said. "Now be ready come Thursday morning."

~3~

Five Seven Five at 30,000 Feet

"My hands are cold," I must have said aloud. As usual I had fallen halfway asleep once the plane hit its plateau and found its jet stream. My state of limbo had worked its way to the level of those mixed place dreams that sneak in and out of the soft murmur-hiss of the plane's hyper-cozy inner-weather. No weather was ever this contrived and thick, I thought as my consciousness battled it out with the murky disposition of my inner night watchman. This is the weather of the devil, and no man or woman in their right mind should be able to tolerate it. Everyone who rides these planes must be 100 % insane.

"Excuse me?" said the girl sitting next to me. She had been mired in her book since right after she buckled her seatbelt. Earlier, on the runway, I had tried to sneak to sneak a peek at the book's title to zero avail.

"Sorry. I was dreaming. Dreaming aloud, I guess," I said through a yawn, my hand over my mouth to shield the girl from my travel breath.

She shut her book. Her boarding pass was her bookmark. *Confessions of Felix Krull*. Thomas Mann. My lush post-slumber disallowed me to make sense of those words at the time. Later on the tarmac in San Antonio I would inform her of how I'd learned how to successfully feign an illness thanks to that book.

"What about?" she asked.

"What about what?" I said stretching each limb as far as my cramped quarters would allow.

"What were you dreaming about?"

"I'm not sure," I said. "Something about ice cream. On the plane—this plane. Yeah, the stewardesses were giving us ice cream. Some other stuff too, but it's all vague. Typical bullshit dream."

"Could be a premonition," the girl said, with a slightly annoying dash of optimism.

"I doubt it. My subconscious is a goddamn mess. And no integrity either. It'd never bless me with anything close to a premonition, ice cream dream or otherwise." A few other details from the dream came forth but nothing worth mentioning. "I seldom dream, and when I do it's usually some tragically forgettable nonsensical whirlwind."

She laughed and loosened her seatbelt so she could face me a little bit. "Either way, the stewardesses in your subconscious are much cooler than the hussies here on Flight 575. Soda, pretzels, finito."

"We got soda and pretzels?" I asked. "I must've been zonked."

"You *were* zonked. I got you pretzels just in case. They keep thinking we're together."

"How'd you remember our flight number? That's kind of spooky. I never remember flight numbers. Don't want to."

"Safety through anonymity," she said.

"The story of my life," I said. My old life, anyway. Not this new one, with its talking static and time travelers and homunculuses. "No, I don't want to know the flight number because then you start thinking about how it'll sound when the news anchors are saying it over and over and over."

"I feel you," she said. "Actually I usually don't remember them. I was just showing off."

"Showing off for me? What do you want to do a thing like that for?"

She skipped over all that and said, "Flight 575. Five seven five. It's easy to remember because of haiku."

"Haiku? Ah, the syllables. Five-seven-five, I gotcha. Are you into haiku?"

"Yes, I am. Well, I just got into it. Recently. Like last week."

"No kidding. What brought it on?"

"I like poetry. I've always liked poetry, both reading it and writing it. But I need rules and regulations. Otherwise I just get carried away with it and don't know when to stop."

"Frogs and lily pads all over the place."

"Yes, exactly. I know you're joking, but that's precisely how it would go down."

Haiku. It'd been a while since I thought about haiku. And to my knowledge I had only written one haiku. Campy little sucker, too. Syllable suicide.

"How many haikus have you written?" I asked her.

"Not many. One a day, for what, like ten days? Ten or twelve. Or eleven. I don't know."

"You write a haiku every single day?"

"That's the plan. One haiku a day. For the rest of my life."

"Wow. You're like a Basho and a half," I said, referencing the only person, place, or thing that I knew about haiku. "That's ambitious."

"It *is* ambitious. It has to be ambitious. I'm mediocre at a lot of things, but I don't excel at any one thing."

"You want to be a haiku champ."

"Yep."

"At a pace of seventeen syllables a day."

"Yes."

"Have you written your haiku for today yet?"

"No, not yet. I was going to write it after I got home and unpacked."

"Empty suitcase, empty mind."

"You got it."

"Well, good luck with that."

What a weird chick. Cool critter, though. And a bona fide cutie. She must've been in her mid-to-late-twenties. Plenty stylish. White turtleneck, dark jeans. Her blondish-brown hair was cut into layers and had a straight-from-the-salon look to it. She seemed to be getting used to having bangs. She was wearing was the same perfume my fourth grade teacher wore. Ms. Bannister. Another weird chick and cool critter. And the only teacher I ever had a legitimate crush on.

"Your ice cream dream…" she said.

"What about it?"

"Was it messy? You said your hands were cold," she said.

Prehistoric now, this dream. "I don't know, I don't remember."

She nodded with the kind of knee-jerk affirmation that indicated the topic was torn and ragged and ready to toss in the dumpster.

I looked down at the slim crimson tie that Deanwood had picked out for me. It was the first time I'd worn one in what I'd guessed to be about ten years and I'd had to go online to learn how to tie the damn thing. Only then, staring down at that tie, did I realize what a ridiculous predicament I had allowed myself to get into; a predicament based on, what else, *faith*. In this case, faith in the belief that the suitcase hovering just above me in the luggage compartment actually possessed a homunculus that I was supposed to give to the world's richest man while he was sleeping in his underground bunker.

"Are you from San Antonio?" the girl asked.

Uh oh. Personal questions. "No, I'm from DC. Quick little trip. Just visiting a friend."

"DC. *Our nation's capital*," she said with feigned grandiloquence. "I've not been to DC since I was itty bitty."

"It's decent enough. A little frumpy, but you have to live somewhere, eh?"

"Allegedly."

"DC's okay," I said. "Pretty even number of haves and have-nots and have-somes and have-lots."

"Sounds like a nice little slice of Mesopotamia."

The plane hit a user-friendly patch of turbulence. The pilot made some brittle wisecracks over the intercom. Tinny pop rock seeped out of someone's headphones.

"How about you? San Antonio or elsewhere?" I asked her.

"I'm from lots of places. San Antonio's sort of my homebase for now."

I'm from lots of places. You and everybody else these days, I thought.

I said to her: "You dig it or nah?"

"Not really. Too hot and too sprawly."

"Grody. Don't like hot, don't like sprawly. You plan on being there forever and ever or…?"

"Who the heck knows," she said, dully.

Indeed. Not me, not her.

"What part of town does your friend live in?" she asked.

"I really have no clue." Anyone who has ever known me well can vouch for my superfluous use of the word "really" when fibbing. "He's supposed to pick me up from the airport. Think he lives somewhere out in the suburbs. It's a big, big city, eh?"

"Not crazy big, but, yeah, it's plenty big."

"I got all kinds of lost driving through it once. Years and years and years ago."

"I get lost there all the time and I live there."

"In retrospect, I'm glad I got lost there," I said, memory kicking in. "I ended up at this Mexican restaurant called La Estrella. Neat little joint. And I tell ya, they got the best chimichanga on the planet. Supernaturally yummy. It's weird, but I swear I can still kind of taste it."

"The chimichanga that time forgot."

"Something like that," I said. "It really was that good. And I'm not a foodie or whatever."

"Supernaturally yummy," she said hitting me gently on the knee for emphasis. I shut my eyes and breathed in her perfume. Ms. Bannister made a cameo in my mind, she was talking about pistons and stems and chlorophyll. The girl shifted in her seat and said in a low, less playful tone: "You know, there could be an explanation for that."

"And explanation for what?"

"For your chimichanga's alleged supernatural yumminess."

I had no response. What a strange thing to say.

"You might have cheated death that day," she said.

Puzzlement in plenitude. "Cheated death?"

"Well, a lot of people believe that the best meal you ever have is the one that you eat right before you die. Ask anyone who's ever had a near death experience what they had that day to eat and they'll all say the same thing: 'I'd just eaten this incredible slice of pepperoni pizza' or 'I'd just had the best chicken pot pie on the planet.'"

"That's odd as heck. A lot of people believe this?"

"Tons. You should befriend a stuntman. The first thing you'll notice about him is that he's got the most boring diet on the planet. A steak tartar or crawfish etouffee could spell disaster for a stuntman. Why do you think astronauts eat that terrible dehydrated astronaut food?"

What was the last meal I had eaten? A meatball sub at Potbelly. And if anything, it was deliciously mediocre at best.

"So by chance I do get a hold of something supernaturally yummy again, what should I do?

"The best thing to do is just lie low until you're hungry enough to eat something else. Don't go anywhere near electrical outlets, stay out of cars or buses, don't even go for a walk. Just take it easy, maybe read a book or watch a movie."

"Sound advice," I said earnestly, though a ring of ambiguous sarcasm snuck out with it. Fortunately, the girl seemed to disregard the statement altogether. Her pupils had zoomed out and locked into place and her lips were frozen in mid-whistle. I took a good long look at her face. It was supposed to have been a round and insipid face but its genetics had been betrayed by the emotive wonder that bubbled just beneath it. She had the kind of beauty that had forced its way onto her features.

"La Estrella," she said finally. "I think I know this place."

"That'd be bad-to-the-bone if you did. And it'd totally confirm I didn't just dream up the joint."

"I do know it, I'm certain. I've actually been there. Once. A long time ago. I had some platter thingy."

What the heck. "Maybe we could check it out sometime, eh?—while I'm in town. We could pretend we're in an episode of The Twilight Zone or something."

This flippant proposition made her get real giddy. "Let's go today!"

I was a bit taken aback by her user-friendliness. "You sure there's only one of them?"

"Pretty sure. We can go online and find out." She went into her thinking mode then said, "We could even go now if you like, when we land. Oh, wait, your friend's picking you up…"

Goddamn imaginary friends. Never did anything for anyone. Time to die, mister…

"Well, I know he's at work and it'd actually probably make his day if I had him pick me up elsewhere later on," I said. "In other words, yeah, let's do it to it."

I almost introduced myself to her when I realized that it was more fun for her to remain a mystery, like time flowing in the middle of the night.

"I'm Dover," she said extending a limp hand.

"Dover?" Had heard her correctly?

"Yes, Dover. Dover Datsun."

"I'm Everett," I said. "Everett Badger." The *Badger* rolled off my tongue with the smoothness of a strafed Panzer.

An older and frowny looking stewardess who I'd not seen yet began pacing up and down the aisle collecting garbage and barking at passengers who hadn't yet put their seats back in their upright positions.

"Are we driving or bussing or cabbing or…?"

"Driving. My car's at the airport."

Weird day gone weirder. Why not. And the next I was to meet Houston's security team for an interview that I was immensely unprepared for yet allegedly had already aced. Time and space had nothing on what was rapidly becoming my status quo.

The frowny old stewardess scolded me for not having my carry-on tucked away. Her fake eyebrows moved up and down with each jab of her pointing finger, which, in turn, was doing all its pointing in synchronicity with the words that were flying out of her mouth. She capped off the routine with a "thanks, sweetie" which was probably meant to smooth the wrinkles out of the ire she'd just blasted me with. The lady and the whole little episode reeked of all things parody.

"Grumpy pants," said Dover.

"Big time grumpy pants," I said. "There's something almost endearing about it, though. Her grumpy doesn't come off as abrasive."

"She's endearingly grumpy."

"There ya go, you nailed it. *Endearingly grumpy.* The Germans must have a word for this."

She loosed an autopilot snicker. I got another dose of her perfume. A realization of sorts was slithering around in my noodle. When it evolved enough to speak, it said: *Hijack this sucker and scoot on back to DC.*

~4~

Stereo Surprises

I didn't hijack it, though. The plane landed on schedule and everyone piled off, troubleshooting with their bags and cell phones. Dover Datsun and I skirted through the airport like we'd known each other for years. We examined the passengers at different gates. The lumpy people were going to St. Louis and the Ghurkas were off to London while the burkas were going to Philly. The people with the fake tans were going back to Buffalo and the people with the real tans were going to Monterrey. The sun-burnt folks were off to Kansas City while the pasty people with no tan at all were bound for Eugene, Oregon. The chrome domes and laptoppers were off to DC, while the Poles and the Germans were going to Chicago. The Quebecois were going to New Orleans while the Greeks slept through their flight to Providence. At least, that's how it all played out in my imagination.

We retrieved our luggage, including the suitcase that Tony had given to me which was supposedly housing Houston's potential homunculus, and then, with the help of some kind of bulky tracking device, we located Dover's car, a little white import with a bumper sticker that read *Jesus is coming – Look busy!*

It was well into autumn but the San Antonio sun was supercharged and inescapable. I took off my blazer for fear of melting inside of it. Dover turned out to be a pretty darn good driver. She wasn't careless but she liked to go fast and did so every opportunity she had. Nor was she indecisive or impulsive, but instead drove with aggressive precision. I was no connoisseur on the art of getaway driving but I would've definitely given her an A plus. Who knows, maybe at that very moment in some parallel universe she was speeding down the highway in a car filled to the sunroof with bags of that parallel universe's currency. I imagined what this scene would look like and I must have snickered.

"Laughing at my driving?"

"Nah, just these residual wacky thoughts from something that happened back in DC," I said. "It's nothing." Ah, so Dover's prowess on the road was the result of some sort of paranoia or self-consciousness, probably induced by a parent or boyfriend or something. Whatever the case, I regretted that she mentioned her driving and feared that she would start to go heavy on the caution.

"Is La Estrella close to the airport?" I asked her. "Time is not an issue or anything, I'm just curious."

"It's kind of close. Relatively, I mean. Nothing is really close to anything in this dumb city," she said. The car glided down the road. I admired Dover's restraint when it came to honking. Car horns were essentially designed to assault people's nervous systems, and I had known many drivers who were obnoxiously trigger-happy with their horns, however Dover cozily abstained when most goobers would probably start blaring their horns and freaking out behind the wheel.

We rode in comfortable silence for a long stretch of minutes, neither one of us offered up the jittery body language that proclaimed the need for small talk or idle remarks on the evanescent San Antonio roadscape. A man in a straw cowboy hat was selling ears of corn for a dollar next to a busted-up phone booth, and a heavily polished super-cab pick-up carrying a trailer full of horses had pulled over to the curb to check him all out. I fiddled with the recline button on my seat and then I leaned back and made palindromes out of car brands and billboard advertisements; the only one that gave me any kind of satisfaction was La Paz/Zap Al, and then Avalon/No lava came along just before my mind strayed elsewhere. I cracked my window and felt the crisp heat of the Texas afternoon. I shut my eyes for a while and momentarily forgot where I was and what I was doing.

My feet made contact with a CD case on the floorboard so I picked it up and scoped it out. Dover Datsun apparently survived on a steady diet of ELO, Led Zeppelin, Boston, Kansas, and Yes.

"Put in whatever you want. Or are you cool with the Supertramp?"

We were indeed listening to *Breakfast in America*. I hadn't noticed. Supertramp. What a weird band.

"This sucker's a time capsule rendered in audio," I said, referring to her CD case.

"I never did make it out of the '70's," Dover said.

"Decent decade to get tangled up in."

"Most people wish they were stuck in the '20's or '30's. For me, it's 1978."

"I'll take the Age of Sail any day of the week," I said.

"Too bad for you San Antonio's landlocked."

Was it? I had no idea. Electrons exist, Brezhnev is a box of bones, and San Antonio is landlocked. *The Logical Song* came on. I had long ago met my *Logical Song* quota so ejected the Supertramp and cued up ELO's *Discovery*. Although I'd not heard it in some time, the first track, *Shine a Little Love*, had hovered in my top twenty songs for nearly three decades.

I braced myself for the song's intro, a long ten seconds of melodramatically triumphant strings and generic marching snare.

… But what I heard instead made me almost upchuck in my hand.

At first I didn't recognize it. It was terrifically loud to the point of causing actual physical pain. Dover swatted at every knob and dial known to man in a frenzied effort to cut the volume.

It was the sound of static. And it was the sound of the *same* static.

It was Kyle again, my friend from the attic, only he didn't sound too friendly this time around. Static seeped out of the car's AC vents and speakers. Dover cannonballed into a Code Red caliber state of panic…

"What did you do?!" yelled Dover.

She pulled the car over, nearly crashing into a motel marquee that read *Clean & Friendly*. She killed the power but the sonic maelstrom persevered. We jumped out and ran a good thirty feet away from the car, and I watched as its automatic windows sank into its doors and Kyle upped his volume to accommodate our new distance. I began to make out individual words within that cacophony: words that only much later in the confines of Houston's bunker—and to my horror—would I successfully piece together.

"Kyle, stop!" I yelled over and over, but Kyle wasn't having any of it.

"Who's Kyle?" said a teenage boy to my left. We had attracted some of the staff from the hotel. They were neither clean nor friendly, as they claimed to be.

"You can't park there. And turn that music down!" this wrinkled lady hollered at us. Her face looked like it had been besieged by Marlboros.

"Turn that off!" said a grimy looking man yielding a broom in a comically threatening manner. "Turn that goddamn music off!"

"It's not music!" I said, dumbly.

Dover sat down on the ground and did one of the few reasonable things one can do in such an aggressively outré scenario. She started crying.

"Turn that music off!" The man took a swipe at me with his broom. I nabbed it from him and for whatever weird reason gave it to the old woman. She gave it back to him, he swiped at me and I took it from him all over again. This time around I tossed it on the motel's roof. It seemed to have been a good decision as the man abandoned us completely and began trying to climb a nearby magnolia tree in an attempt to get up on the roof to fetch it.

"I'm callin' the cops," the woman said.

"Easy, easy. We'll split as soon as we fix our car. Okay? Just cool off."

"Turn that music off!" yelled the man from the thick of the tree. Magnolia trees were practically designed for climbing and from where I stood it looked like the man would be on the roof at any moment. Then he did something unexpected of him. He fell.

"Jay!" said the woman, "Oh, no…"

"I'm alright," he said, but he wasn't alright. "I'm alright."

I sat down next to Dover and put my arm around her back. We bathed in Kyle's fury until he finally reduced his presence to a high-pitched nearly subsonic sliver. The woman attended to her banged-up crony. They both eventually went back inside.

Dover and I sat in silence watching cars go by.

"Proggiest Prog-rock ever," I said. "Makes ELO sound like Saturday morning cartoons." Actually, a lot of ELO did kind of sound like Saturday morning cartoons.

"Why were you saying 'Stop, Kyle' over and over? Who is Kyle?" Dover said.

"I was saying that?"

"You know you were saying that. You were yelling 'Stop, Kyle' over and over and over," Dover said. "Jesus, what *was* that? I saw like electric looking smoke or something." On top of being thoroughly confused, Dover was beginning to get angry and indignant. Rough seas, this stuff. Nothing but whitecaps and dorsal fins. I froze up and said nothing.

Again she asked who Kyle was, and after a husky little bout of silence, I said, "Have you ever had someone try to explain something to you that they themselves did not fully understand? It's 100% unfun and equally unenlightening."

She picked up a pine cone and launched it at her car. It soundlessly disappeared into the car's interior. She turned to me and said, "Let's go to La Estrella. Mexican food always gives me clarity."

"It always gives me something, too, but it ain't clarity."

Silence and a frown. Duly noted: Dover Datsun was immune to grandpa jokes.

"Can you drive? My nerves are nutso," Dover said.

"Yeah, no sweat, as long as you do all the navigating."

We sat there until our collective composure came back around and then we walked over to her car and took off.

~5~

La Estrella and Mr. Catbirddog

It turned out to be the same La Estrella, complete with same menu—including beef chimichangas—and the same small congenial staff. I thought it was heretical that we were the only customers in the restaurant, granted we were in that limbo between lunch and dinner. I ordered a Dos XX and a mescal—when you're off the wagon, you're off the wagon—and Dover ordered the same. The chips and salsa were incredible, even after Dover buried the chips in salt.

To my surprise, the staff remembered me. I'd led myself to believe that their food was undeniably incredible and any hungry patron would've responded in the same manner that I did that day long ago. I also believed that any staff capable of producing such wonderful food must also be very capable at other facets of life, including remembering and distinguishing the faces of their patrons. Nonetheless, I was impressed. I walked over to the kitchen window and doused them in accolades with my "kitchen Spanish".

"They remember you," said Dover as I sat back down. "And they seem to adore you. Wild stuff."

"Conditional love, this bunch. I tipped 'em like a thousand percent."

I spied a portrait on the wall near the entrance. It was titled *Los Hermanos de La Estrella.* It took me little time to realize it was a portrait of the staff, all six of them, brothers, as I now understood them to be, mustachioed and young, displaying their usual unadulterated pleasantry. The portrait was amateurish at best, which only added to its charm. I liked to believe that it was painted by a seventh brother, possibly too young to work around the restaurant or whose artistic temperament the other six brothers preferred to have remain untainted by the daily miasma of the kitchen.

"Salud," said Dover clinking her Dos XX to mine, "What should we toast to?"

"I'll bet poor Basho hasn't gotten a toast in a while."

"To Basho?"

"To Basho." More clinks from the glasses.

"Could I hear one of your haikus?" I asked.

"Hmm, I'm not so sure. I've got them all written down. Wait, I've got one…"

"Let 'er rip."

"Best gift from Japan: Not some fire-breathing T-rex, but good ol' Haiku."

"Ha! I love it!"

"First haiku I wrote, must have been ten years ago, it's kind of silly."

"That's a very good first haiku. No mention of frogs or lily pads. I'm impressed."

"Still, very silly. I'm much more serious now, big juicy topics."

"That's a good strategy. Save the frogs and lily pads until you're old and all washed up."

She took a big pull from her Dos XX. Our empty chip basket was snatched up and replaced with one that had a glistening crew seemingly straight from the fryer.

"Have you ever been to Mexico?" I asked.

"Only all the time. Literally once a week. My work demands it."

"What is it that you do? Besides write haiku."

"It's kind of like Kyle, I could try to explain it, but it wouldn't work."

Before I could respond to her, one of the brothers dropped off our chimichangas. "Very hot! Muy caliente!"

I studied my plate with anticipation. The chimichanga sat diagonally and was covered in chili con carne and melted Monterrey jack cheese, a dab of both guacamole and sour cream sat on a pile of shredded lettuce and high tide of yellow rice had worked its way up to the top of the chimichanga. I wondered if Brezhnev had ever eaten a chimichanga.

"You prepared for this?" she said. "Need some time alone or anything?"

"Negative, chica. Dig in at will."

The chimichanga was hot, and as I was blowing on it I noticed for the first time there were other patrons in the restaurant: two men in trenchcoats, standing just in front of the portrait at the entrance, motioning at...me?

Dover noticed too. "Is that your friend?"

Neither one was my imaginary friend. The men were both very large and their trenchcoats did little to conceal their ex-football player frames. The only thing about their physique that lacked a life of athletics was the color of their skin: a bleached white. Their stony chins were moving up and down and I realized they were whispering to each other.

They walked over to our table.

"You're Badger."

"You're early."

"Weren't we supposed to be seeing you tomorrow, Badger?"

"Today's not tomorrow, is it?"

"No, it ain't, Vigo. It's definitely still today."

"So why's this Badger here, it being today and not tomorrow?"

"I don't know. Why don't you ask him?"

"Why you here now, Badger?"

"That's a good lookin' chimi. You ever seen a chimi look that good, Milly?"

"No, not ever."

"I guess since you're here, Badger, you might as well get to work."

"You're packing light, Badger."

"Your stuff in the car? I bet his stuff's in his car."

"You mean *her* car."

"Miss, you ought to pack that up and eat it at home."

"How do you say 'to-go box' in Mexican?"

"Miss, you mind popping your trunk so Badger can nab his belongings?"

"Let that chimi cool first, Badger. Either that or douse it in guacamole and sour cream."

I saw movement to my left, outside the window, near one of the two cacti that flanked the La Estrella's marquee. Check that, the movement wasn't near the cacti, it *was* one of the cacti: the cactus on the left had begun *walking* toward the entrance to the restaurant.

The two trenchcoats watched me watch the cactus. They turned around and said "Catbirddog!" in synchronized exclamation.

The cactus struggled with the door a bit. Actually, it struggled for an embarrassing amount of time, and it continued to struggle until our ever-so-alert server took it upon himself to help the poor fellow out. The cactus then entered, wiped his feet—he did have feet, I noticed, feet that were inside of a pair of blue Nike tennis shoes—and then he moseyed over to the table, bumping into every possible table, chair, piñata, fake cactus, host stand, and gumball machine in between.

"You two, scram. I see you again it's too soon," the cactus said.

"Boss, we're only lookin' out for you."

"I'm not your boss anymore, remember? You work for Badger here now," he said in a voice heavily muffled by the thickness of the cactus costume. I say costume but the damn thing looked real enough. I wanted to test the sharpness of its needles but refrained.

"Badger, meet Millicent and Vigo, two biggest bozos east of the Pacific and west of Planet X. If you can guess which is which, I'll pay for that chimi. Ha! Like *I* even know." The two trench coats actually offered their hands to me and I complied; their grips were heavy and firm but both offered slippery evidence of having recently held some Mexican dish. Dover was frozen in befuddlement. Her eyes darted slowly back and forth like she was watching some amateur ping-pong match.

"I'm Mr. Catbirddog. I used to be you, now you're me. Houston gave me some fancy parting gifts to offer some advice to you so that's what I'm doing here. What size cactus do you wear? Ha, ha, ha, not really, I made this myself. Head of security means master of disguise, but you already know about all that shit. Ok, advice from the master, here we go. First, Houston stinks. Literally. Bastard doesn't wipe so don't go near him unless you have to. Second, Houston don't sleep so good. You wanna be sneaky and grab a smoke or something then make sure you spike his cran-apple with something heavy. I recommend Nyquil, the red kind, cherry or whatever. Third, nobody in the world is out to get Houston but he's still a paranoid fuck. The only security does any kind of work around here are those spoiled brats with all them computers over in Austin. Easy job, kid. Buy lots of big books and a good-sized flashlight. I recommend a ton-and-a-half of porn as there ain't no womenfolk on the payroll. Fourth, don't tell nothin' to the elevator boy. Actually, I'll pay you ten grand cash right now if you promise to sucker punch that little fruitcake for me. Fifth, you get a chopper, not a goddamned hog but a whirlybird kinda chopper; best thing to do is hire yourself a pilot. Don't go tryin' to fly that thing by yourself, right fellas?"

"Aye, aye, boss!"

"You taking notes, Badger? Maybe your lady friend here's got a good memory. *Jeez*, am I sweatin'. This thing's hotter than two minks screwin' in a wool boot. Fellas, you wanna show Badger here to the elevator? I gotta lose this cactus before I go up in flames."

"Aye, aye, boss!"

"Don't call me that no more, I'm retired. No more Houston for me. Badger, tell that regal fuck to hit up the right account this time. Thanks to that fuck's lousy memory, some asshead in Switzerland ended up being able to afford half of Hispaniola—the *good* half! And make sure he sends me the right amount. Loan him some fingers if he needs 'em. OK, I'm out of here. Remember, don't press the red button. Press the red button and the whole planet goes boom, except for Texas. Ha, ha, not really."

I watched Catbirddog as he made his way for the door, looking like a big green pointy pinball. He cursed indecipherably and grumbled through his cactus suit while the server opened the door for him again.

I looked up at the two trench coats and made a time-out motion for whatever reason. Then I ate my chimichanga. It tasted unbelievable. Dover took a bite of hers and was visibly delighted. Every time Vigo or Millicent interrupted I threw a chip at them. This went on until Dover and I were finished, and then I bought Vigo and Millicent four orders of fried ice-cream and paid our tab. Dover and I walked out to her car to fetch my luggage out of the trunk.

"You're a flesh-and-blood cuckoo clock, mister," she said.

"It's a recent development. I was 95% normal up until November."

"You roll with a weird crew."

"Who, those dudes? They're not my crew."

"Who's your crew then? Is Kyle part of your crew?"

"No, Kyle is not part of my crew. I don't have a crew. And I don't know what Kyle is. He's either God or a trickster spirit that would like for me to believe that he's God. I don't really know which."

"I don't get it all. Not one bit of it."

"I know it sounds absurd. It *is* absurd. It's all absurd."

"We could compensate by having a very normal goodbye," she said.

"Super slim chance there."

"Let's try. I bet we can do it," she said extending her hand. "Goodbye, Everett."

"Adios, Dover," I said, grasping her hand. It was surprisingly hard and calloused.

"And thank you," she said. The sun was tumbling toward the world behind her. The early evening glare assaulted my eyeballs.

"How do we do this again? Serendipity's about as predictable as a sprayed roach."

"I'm the only Dover Datsun on the planet. I've checked. Look me up sometime."

"I'll do that. Maybe sooner than later," I said just before she kissed me. I tasted the salt from the chips on her lips and then I tasted the heavenly mystery that supplies the ballast for our whims and dreams. I held her close and tight and a lone tear perched itself in my eye, a tear not for her, but for the partings of both my past and future that she personified.

She handed me a piece of paper.

"What's this?"

"A present, rendered in five-seven-five."

I was about to unfold it when she tackled me with kisses again, misdirected kisses with much movement and sound. "Stay cool, fool," she said finally. Then she got into her car and coolly sped off into the chrome motion of the San Antonio traffic.

I watched her little car until it blended in with its brethren, and then I unfolded the paper and looked at the words she'd written there with sneaky and haphazard handwriting....

Just like certain stars
We add and subtract from life
With no awareness

~6~

The Madness in Flannels

"What's the word, bird?" asked the elevator boy, a tiny mustachioed bundle of nervous energy. He had badges and medals all over the front of the heavily tailored dress jacket of his maroon uniform.

"You a major or a general?" I asked, taking the freedom to finger one of his medals.

"These I got from the boss. Good conduct awards," he said in a comically high-pitched voice that was entirely too loud for the crypt-like elevator. "So what did he say to you? I gotta know." The man had a deterrent a makeup as any I'd ever met. He looked remarkably like a rat. Shifty posture, oblong head, beady eyes; all he was missing was some fur and a tail.

"What'd who say to me?"

"Catbirddog," the man said. "C'mon, I gotta know."

"He offered me decent dough to sucker punch you," I said.

"He did, eh? Guess he's still sore at me not being able to keep what's bouncing around in my brain from making friends with my mouth. It's like the boss is out to lunch in here. Nobody at the helm of things."

The elevator was seemingly going down fast but there was no indication of how many floors we were passing by. The elevator boy apparently only had to deal with two buttons: a big red one with an arrow pointing up and a big blue one with an arrow pointing down.

"Nicky," he said, offering his itty bitty hand. "You're Badger, right? I'm Nicky the elevator boy. *Badger*. That's a really funny name. Never met a Badger. Met a Parrot—two Parrots, come to I think of it—Jim and Chip and they wasn't brothers neither. Met a Fox, met a Swan, met a…oh, what was his name? Bruce…Panda!—yep, met a Panda. Never a Badger, though. Real funny name, Badger. That really your real name?"

"Nope. I made it up. My real last name's Pufferfish."

"Zing! Good one, mister."

"How far beneath the ground are we?"

"Couple a thousand feet."

"How far down are we going?"

"Three-thousand feet and change. Or do you do the metric? You look the metric type, Mr. Pufferfish. Totally cool if you ware. I'm a worldly man, too, you know, worldly and worry free: that's Nicky in a nutshell," he said and inched closer. "He really say sucker punch me?"

"No, he said to tell you 'hi'. Actually, his exact words were: 'Tell Nicky I said hey.'"

"Really? I didn't think he'd be that forgiving with me. He seems to be the, you know, the grudge type, that Catbirddog. That's cool, though. Tell him I said hey back if ya seem him."

"Will do...Is this me?" I said as the door opening revealing a non-descript looking stretch of carpeted corridor.

"Yep. Just follow the singin'. It'll take you where you want to go."

"The singing?"

"Yeah, the *singin'.*"

I gathered my two suitcases and stepped off the elevator. The floor was heavily padded and I sunk what must have been two inches into the carpet. "Why so soft?" I said.

"For protection purposes. Enhances the odds of, whaddya call it?—*longevity.* You have a good day now, Mr. Pufferfish."

"Okay, Nicky," I said as I reached down and pressed into the carpet with my hand. The elevator doors closed with a slight whir and a dull thud, and then I was alone.

The corridor was illuminated by a seemingly invisible source of light, as there were no bulbs, lambs, or phosphorescent lights to be seen anywhere. I only had one option concerning which way to walk: straight ahead, which offered a view of nothing but more of what appeared to be an endless corridor. As I walked along, the silence gave way to an implosion of recent memory. I thought of Dover and her sweet nostalgic scent and I thought of the event in the car with Kyle. Why had he assaulted us like that? There was nothing tricksterish about that at all. It was simply surprising and terrifying and nothing came out of it for any us. Then I thought of the words that were jumbled within that long moment: Kyle had said I had a puppy? I'm sure he had said something about a puppy. But I didn't have a puppy. And I wouldn't have a puppy. I hated dogs and hadn't owned one since childhood.

I frowned to myself and carried on with the suitcases, one in tow and the other one—the one which supposedly cradled the homunculus—in hand. I'd gone all of thirty feet when I heard what Nicky must have been talking about: I heard the sound of someone singing. It was distant and unintelligible, but loud enough for me to discern that the source was not lacking in enthusiasm, as well as a heavy disregard for professional training. I carried along with speed until the garbled hollering offered actual words…

- *Thy choicest gift in store!*

- *On her be pleased to pour!*

There were no doorways on either side of the corridor and the source of the singing seemed to come from the corridor itself. And then far ahead, in slump, was a new development in the stretch of corridor.

- *Long may she reign!*

- *May she defend our laws! (cough, cough)*

My anticipation and my disdain for the unvaried austerity took control of me and I ran hurriedly toward this odd little pocket of variance.

- *And ever give us cause!*

- *To sing with heart and voice!*

What I approached was a thick pile of red and blue flannel with a man inside of it, an Englishman, I soon gathered, and a very elderly and noisome one at that.

Dallas Austin Houston paused mid-song and looked at me with impartial brevity before his heavily-lidded eyes went on to address the floor.

"Did you know, Badger, that your beloved P-51 Mustang, the same one you so valiantly and courageously defended your bombers over Germany with, was equipped with a *Rolls-Royce* engine?"

His face had a wayward handsomeness about it, his rigid jaw and muscular frame had been overtaken by the accrued lumpiness of late age and various red patches crept about his exposed skin. A thin tuft of grey sat mussed on his head and his eyebrows had an extra-dimensional bushiness. His flannels sheathed what I could only imagine to be a grotesquely corpulent sprawl. Houston smelled of hospital.

"Yes, sir, I did know that. But I'm an Army guy, sir. Means nothing to me."

"Yes, yes, of course. The A-10 was your craft, as I remember. The 'Tank Killer' with its Gatling gun; quite a bit of antiquated weaponry to equip an aerocraft with, don't you think? I'm led to believe it served your country better in its internal disputes more so than within the imperial realm that it's so recently grown accustomed to. Why, I'd say a *Chicagoan* might be quicker to label that particular piece of weaponry a scourge before any Arab or Chinaman."

"Well, I'd say its modern day effectiveness trumps any of its antiquity or, uh, ambiguous usage in the past, sir," I ad-libbed.

"Nonetheless, that plane has been retired, I believe."

"It was retired, yeah, but not before it had its day."

"Indeed, Badger, indeed. I'm sure given time I could round you up a number of fencers who would proclaim as much for their sport." He spat this last word out of his mouth and I watched as a globular piece of the gelatinous Englishman shimmied down the wall.

"Badger, would you be so kind as to help me up? Careful, I seemed to have gotten a little upchuck on my sleeve there. I have simple requests, Badger. I dictate a very simple list of the most meager of necessities to those who assist me and I still find myself clutching the same defiant brands of Kentucky bourbon."

"Well, I'll be able to help you out with the bourbon, sir."

"Perhaps I'd allow you to oblige if we were neighbors in a University of Texas dormitory. However, your position demands you keep some distance from the *Kickin' Chicken* or whatever else you may be so unmerciful as to offer me. I assure you, Badger, that you will be far too preoccupied with the more immediate demands of your, *hup*, position to warrant recommendation concerning my, *hup*, vices. You have met with Mr. Catbirddog? I'm sure he has informed you of the alliance between the more benthic elements involving the fan base of the Serbian football club, Red Star Belgrade, and their antipathy toward my accomplishments? I wonder, then, Mr. Badger, if I may inquire whether you think we should continue with my plan to install the de-atomizer underneath that wretched place of their worship, the Red Star Stadium, or whether you would find it preferable to follow the advice of that man that you are replacing, Mr. Catbirddog, and wait a couple years 'til the technology gets a little bit better."

"I say we build the thing."

"Oh, goody," he said just before his mouth filled with vomit; his cheeks deflated slowly and, to my disgust, I realized he was swallowing the whole mess back down in patient little gulps.

"Forgive me, Badger. I've already mentioned my assistants and their, *hup*, ill taste in spirits. Even the alliterative ring of *Maker's Mark* eludes them as they head straight with confidence for the *Old Featherhead*."

Houston was now leaning with his back to the wall and I watched as he inched downward back into his original position.

"Tell me, Badger, in the sport of basketball, rather than extending the length of the athlete, why do they not simply *lower the net?*"

Houston turned his head to his side and shut his eyes. I wasn't sure what he wanted from his question but my lips started moving anyway.

"It's evolution, sir. I'm sure the archer fish would rather have lungs or wings, or perhaps even just the ability to subsist on a vegetarian diet, but as it is, he has to spit water at his prey in order to persist. It's just how it happened, sir."

"You bring evolution into the matter, well, then, surely you won't be surprised when such a sport is rendered extinct."

"Makes no difference to me, sir."

"Yes, of course, with your baseball and your football, of course it makes sense to me that you would prefer the company of the do-do bird and the passenger pigeon to that of the trilobite."

He rolled his head back toward me and looked me up and down with his bulbous, reddened eyes.

"Badger, frankly, I'm disappointed. The one characteristic I would expect from the least competent heads-of-security is the ability to notice nuances in your immediate surroundings. The case in this particular point being the very recent happenings concerning the suitcase at your feet."

I looked to my feet and felt something that I'd not felt since my easily-spooked childhood: the heights of adrenaline. The suitcase that was carrying the homunculus had managed to abandon the vertical position that I'd left it in and now sat on the floor stirring with motion. The zipper of the suitcase was now moored at its base and the thing inside began to make its way out...

"Well, go on then, Badger...Let's see what they've got for me!"

The homunculus slowly emerged from the bag and into our view, but it wasn't at all as I'd imagined the thing to be. It wasn't a sharp-eyed humanoid with an oversized head, nor was it slick with membrane and cloaked in transparent skin streaked with veins...The homunculus wasn't a homunculus at all: it was something else, something furry and familiar...

"A puppy," I must have said.

"No, it's not a puppy, you goddamned fool! It just looks and acts like a puppy. And yet, it's impossible...I only made one of these. This very one!—1936, it was. I sold it to a Negro gentleman in Catalonia, dapper fellow, didn't speak a lick of Catalan."

The adorably spotted oddity then sniffed its way over to its new master.

The thing in your suitcase, Kyle had said from the stereo system of Dover's car, the thing in your suitcase is a puppy, but the puppy is really…

And then the bomb exploded.

Dover Datsun had learned of the assassination by way of BBC radio. Houston had been killed by a small bomb inside of the subterranean bunker where he had lived for the previous twenty-five years, a sum that amounted to nearly a quarter of his life. So far, Houston had been the only death that was reported and authorities were conducting interviews to determine how the bomb had found its way into his bunker and apparently onto his lap. Dallas Austin Houston had recently made news for his reneging of a controversial thirty-million dollar contribution to the Cyclical Night, an Argentinean-based group of fringe scientists that had claimed to have perfected and copyrighted the world's first time travel machine. Reports indicate that when asked why he cancelled his more than generous offer to the group after only one installment, he replied, "Because I would have better chance of going back and forth in time on top of Herbert George Wells's tombstone than in that aluminum whoopee cushion they built with my money!"

Dover was then interrupted by a familiar yet unlikely sound. The shutters were acting up, she thought. The wind's got a hold of the shutters again. She looked out at the smooth placidity of the merlot sea. She no longer marveled at the porpoises. She'd gotten used to them being around, like Americans do with squirrels, or Albanians do with wild dogs. Actually she was beginning to find their presence almost annoying. Who cares if you're still in the ocean? And why didn't you come on land when everyone else did? The unlikely sound came around again, this time solidifying its presence in the world—in Dover's world. Too rhythmic for wind, she thought. She took a sip of Dominican rum and pressed *save* on her laptop. Then she opened the file called Spare Parts. *Too rhythmic for wind*. Poetic, and even five syllables. She felt a flash of something like optimism as she placed it there underneath the other rogues and orphans, the mingled slivers of cosmos-turned-text by way of her sandy, somnambulistic treks.

Dover then did something she did with increasingly less frequency: She stood up, mainly because one of her legs had fallen asleep, but also because she needed to go answer the door.

~~~~~~

Part 2: Uncertain Stars

"One day, when you least expect it, your video won't play after that ad." – Glenmont Noseworthy, Futurist-in-Residence for the FBI

~1~

Purgatory

Between the derelict memory of my yesteryear and the misty yet-to-be I was left straining for a set of trustworthy coordinates. In the meantime I drifted around my ten acres of stratosphere and ate French toast and scrambled eggs at 2am. I was a tiny spot in the southern sky, an avatar for reality's penumbra, and lurking in its most opaque stratum; a renegade jester glossing the world up in nice hue of bafflement—not the thirty day wash-out, but permanent.

I injected question marks like a blotter of acid, instilling doubt in those who think that's really just dirt and clay beneath their feet. I was an antidote to the tethered dogmas we've nibbled on for dusty years, reeking of reality's bare evanescence, and stuffed with every bit of its inherent sorrow. Part of my job was to offer these symptoms to others. It's like painting a nuclear missile, or styling up a corpse: seemingly unnecessary, but something that's just got to be done.

I did not know why I was where I was. I was positive, though, that I didn't care much for finding out. Something lingered beyond this assigned position of mine, and I was pretty sure whatever it was had claws and fangs. Consequently my life was a steady diet of *avoidance*. I dismissed thinking about the events of my life that did or did not happen, those flickering happenings that placed me where I was, and I moved cautiously from day to day while secretly bracing myself for inevitable surprise. It's easy, live and learn, only take it easy on the *learn* part.

Except I did learn one thing. I learned that if you know too much, if you find out too much, they come after you. That's what happened to me. You have to hope that the other guys get to you first and shuffle up your identity, maybe dose you with the same set up I had, which was some sort of honest-to-God witness protection program. Let me explain: This has nothing to do with the Mafia, the CIA, the FBI, or any other tailored bugaboo in a Crown Victoria. That's all kiddy pool in comparison. Hell, it ain't even kiddy pool—it's upchucking on your nanny's lap. This has to do with the vaporous uprights that float through doors, the bleeding palms that straddle the equator, the shiny, spherical zigzags that swallow Cessnas, the furry afterimage that walks like a man… This has to do with what's before and after science, this has to do with the original Untouchables, this has to do with ontology and question marks, this has to do with *playing God*.

I wasn't always like this, I know. I wasn't always so nebulous, so bouncy-eyed, and so controversial. In fact I was once a connoisseur of the *physical*, a paradigm of belief in the undeniable factish meat of good ol' reality. I knew up from down, left from right, maybe even at some point right from wrong. That all changed once they got a hold of me. They turned everything upside-down and then tossed me through the ceiling I used to park my shoes on. As a result my psychological makeup was like a Chinese ping-pong tournament: Advanced and intriguing, but not really something you'd want to be part of.

Who I had become: Captain Badger Quartermile, head of security at the world's first fully functional stratospheric airport, the Jules Verne Stratoport, also known as JVS, and also known, mainly by its jaded, spacey inhabitants, as Purgatory. You've probably heard of JVS. It used to pop up in the news all the time, and it's still all over those online science magazines. Not so much of because of what it's done, but what it's capable of doing—and any day now, they say. The hegemonic apex of the most potentially devastating scenario charts?—that's JVS. Oh, it's king, alright. It's lapped the volcanoes, the fault lines, the radio-free tsunami bait crust communities and then some. Tomorrow's atomic fireball and everyone can feel it in their bones. It's the new Hindenburg—only bigger and better!

I had been there for a years, but I wasn't exactly sure how many. The record books on me were blank, and my superiors ignored my inquiries.

The gut of my job was to oversee the arrivals and departures of passengers, usually an obnoxiously affluent breed that preferred the novelty of stratospheric flight exchange—that is, swapping planes at over 100,000 feet on a floating airport. My colleagues and I supplied them with the travel of the future as they had always wished it to be: risky, expensive, and unnecessary, but goddamned *futuristic*.

I spent most of my days pointing a lot and spewing instructions to passengers as they were ephemerally shuffled through the corridors of this place that was no place, this discus platform, stationary in all practical regards, that heftily floated 19.2 miles above the Tropic of Capricorn in the western hemisphere. JVS was an oblong metal island that owed it appearance to the neglected design of the early twentieth century's science fiction (I am all too aware that my workplace was a temporary celebration of the capability of humanity to *proceed*, even if by a means that displays comical and ill-advised stretches of exaggerated technology).

My position was technically composed of three parts: Travel Exchange Director of Corridor Divisions, the aforementioned Head of Security, and Chief of Ambience. The latter the result of my superior's belief that I was a primary component in generating the feeling of otherworldliness, abstraction, and marvel that a floating airport ought to possess. My impression was a crucial one mainly because I had a hell of a lot of presence there (I recall obligatory viewings of *Brazil* and *the Fifth Element* during the Style and Behavior phase of my training). For safe measure I instructed my employees to refer to me as Lord Vader while in the company of non-personnel.

The passengers arrived in mingled clumps, each of them equipped with a peachy enthusiasm soon muffled by the brutalist web of pipes and tubes of the entry corridor. If that didn't widen their eyes, then the chronic whirring sound and omnipresent, clinical whiteness of the station's interior certainly did. I watched them trundle along my wall, projected there from the surveillance cameras in the corridor. Lesser officers did my dirty work as I sipped my morning coffee.

Morning: A weightless word as far as I was concerned.

My mornings, afternoons, and evenings had long ago given up their distinctions. They seeped into each other until the obligations that they summon deemed themselves interchangeable. I simply had *time*: a steady flow of it, chopped up to my liking.

For better or worse, I could show up to work whenever I wanted. I opted to stay in bed and listen to music, at least until guilt showed up to spur me over to the terminal. I was working my way through David Bowie's *Low*. The first album of the "Berlin trilogy" as it became to be known. *Low* was the first of Bowie's three collaborations with producer, Brian Eno, as an expat in cold war Berlin. *Low* was to help solidify Bowie's position among the avant-garde, as well as swiftly remove him from the U.S. charts. It was his first dab at making music that channeled the spirit of the information age. It was his *Zooropa* before *Zooropa*.

One of the better instrumentals on that album, *A New Career in a New Town*, seeped through the pores of my ceiling and I wiggled my toes to its tiny synthetic thump.

The notorious Master Blaster was in idle purr beneath my bed. The Master Blaster was a remote-controlled car that, with not much benefit of doubt, resembled a shiny little horseshoe crab. A camera atop its spoiler enabled me to operate from any video screen of my choosing. The big red button on the remote made the Master Blaster shoot two feet of flame out of its nostrils. I played with the thought of giving it a run through the corridor, frightening the passengers as I've done so many times before, but the idea lost its swagger, and I gave way to Bowie and staying horizontal.

I dozed intermittently until my bladder suggested I get things going. I chugged the remainder of my tepid coffee and wreaked some havoc on my bathroom. Then I splashed my face with cold water, dressed, and fled the cramped, metallic drapery of my living quarters.

I ambled over to Best Pancake World, a diner whose only decent trait was its proximity to my living quarters. As usual the place was wall to wall with sybaritic bubble butts from every industrialized corner of the globe. I glided by the hostess, a Chilean gal with bright turquoise hair, and took the small table in the corner. I stretched and yawned for a while, and then put my selective-hearing to good use. The waiter, a Pakistani named Surfy, cruised by, leaving a wake of imposter *Obsession*. He swiveled and glared at me from underneath his bushy unibrow. I produced a bag of honey-roasted peanuts from my pocket and began to munch on them—the only thing that more repellent than the service in this place was the food in this place.

The place was packed with smiles for miles spouting fragmented highlights of the life of travel: tales of consequence-free mischief in the Mr. Bordellos of that rotten city below us, on the *good* side of the wall—far, far away from the bang and the clatter of the city's Adolescent Zone (a moniker of murky origin. Some claim it's due to the fifteen or so years that the area has existed on area maps, while others suggest it reflects the average age of its violent, sinewy ingredients).

A severely tanned American man in a fedora was telling a much younger yet equally tanned woman about a "premeditated nostalgia tour" he took in Brazzaville.

"A fucking bumpy-ass cab ride, a goddamned what-do-you-call-it—a *Polaroid* camera, a fucking tape recorder, you know, like a cassette…and this small vial thing that had this, like, perfume or something in it that smelled just like the inside of the goddamned cab."

The man couldn't have been in any hurry but he still loosed his words into the world with the erratic spillage of a man at the gallows.

"What did the inside of the cab smell like?"

"Straight-up dookie."

"Ew, you should've totally got out and walked."

"Oh, I was tempted for sure. It stunk real bad… It was like this, like, air-freshener or something, vanilla air-freshener and, like, three hundred years of cigarette smoke and big time body odor."

This segued into a conversation about bars in Kuala Lumpur where your drinks are made (and spilled) by clever little gibbons with bowties and vests, and eventually a conversation about money.

JVS was just another chip on the bat for these people, an obligatory pit-stop for the perma-tourists that were draped around me slinging anecdotes with parched voices and rotten breath, a verbal nest of hassling times where the appeal thrived only in the retrospect.

I folded the drink menu into a pointy little paper airplane. I didn't really know what else to do with it so I threw it at the waiter who was a couple of tables over taking an order and speaking German while nodding his head a lot. The Germans, a duo of nuclear families it seemed, were all wearing dark-framed rectangular eye-glasses. They were also all frowning. A fat kid beyond them sitting backwards in his chair saw me throw the plane and began to smile and wave. I waved back and surveyed my table for more potential armament.

A majority of the customers here were pretty husky, as were most of the passengers at the station. I shut my eyes and listened to their curled-up voices toss out the news. They talked about which countries no longer sold batteries, cities where ordering *la fourure du Mickey* got you a plateful of deep-fried rat, they talked about airlines that sold parachutes, places where car alarms serenaded intruders with Michael Jackson's *Beat It*. This is my routine, this is my job: dealing with these mediocre lumps of choppy limbs and mild sins and then sending them on their way.

I realized that I wasn't in any sort of mood to be where I was so I jetted for the door. The fat kid started waving again so I gave him the finger. The entrance was bloated with passengers and all their stupid gear so I had to squeeze by walking sideways, hands together pointy in mock prayer. I winked at the hostess but she did not wink back. Someone's travel bag tripped me up and I nearly fell.

Even though I am a supervisor, I have a supervisor: Bentley. He was at the counter eating jelly beans. He spotted me and wrote something on his hand. A colorful fact for you: Bentley had no testicles. He had had them removed to stifle "instinctual distraction"— a move which didn't expedite any pity or understanding from my part. Bentley was a head case. Without his testicles he was even more of a head case, and certainly more prone to distraction, albeit of the non-instinctual variety. Bentley gave up sex to make silent movies with a hand held camera on a floating airport. The 21st century's very own Sidney Olcott, only asexual, deranged, sans viewership, and most importantly, *ozonal*. Bentley could, however, fight. He was a severe martial arts man, and he spoke frequently of youthful travels to eastern plateaus to seek higher elevation and a steady diet of cabbage with a man name Lao Tse. Bentley had a long slim beard until three weeks ago.

I instinctively floated over to the main terminal and high-fived Ms. Maps, my assistant. She started to spin around on her stool with the disposition of a bored kid, her feet shuffling along the stool's foot rest, crablike. The motion slightly increased the volume of her blonde 60's sci-fi hair and I stole eyefuls of soft upper thigh with each revolution.

"How's my favorite whirlybird?"

"Crummy. We're about to be invaded by about two-hundred Texans. Texans from Dallas, the really *Texas* part of Texas," she said.

"Yippee-yi-yo."

"Where have you been?"

"I was in Best Pancake World not eating again. That waiter wants to chop my head off."

"He'd probably like you more if you didn't throw peanuts at him."

"I didn't today and he was still mean. You smell good, like berries. Not strawberry, not raspberry, not blueberry..."

"Vanilla."

"Ah."

She shifted her momentum and eventually came to a stop. Then poked her legs out one by one and pulled her white tights back up, starting with the ankle and working her way up to her thigh. It was a little shimmy that she routinely encored with.

"Why the parka?" she asked. "Expecting rain?"

"It's not a parka. I've never owned a parka. It's a..." I raised my arms and checked myself out. "...What do you call these?"

Ms. Maps was not her real name. Her blood name was Greta Ray Garrett, a splendid name muted by the slang of the station. "Maps" was a reference to the tattooed maps that covered her upper arms and shoulders (that her white turtleneck usually concealed). Maps of subway systems: New York, London, Paris, Moscow, DC, Montreal, Mexico City, Chicago's El, Boston's T, and Berlin's U-Bahn. Ms. Maps aspired to have every heavy rail system on her body. She had three Pomeranians named Bart, Marta, and Septa. I slept with her about once every two weeks.

She said, "You call them parkas."

"You want to open the door? Do I look weird enough?"

"You look plenty weird. Wait, do that thing where you scrunch your face up. Perfecto. You ready?"

"Yeah, I'm ready... This really a parka? Remember, don't smile or show your teeth, they'll interpret it as a sign of hostility. Stare down and haunch your shoulders like this."

"Yuk yuk yuk. Okay, here we go, I'm pressing the button."

She pressed the button. Texans came and went...

Half an hour later I asked, "Who's next?"

"Small party, on a Learjet out of Washington, DC," said Ms. Maps.

"Party like party, or party like group?"

"Party like party."

"Important or expendable?"

"The people or the party?"

"The people. The party people."

"Uncertain."

What I did remember: a smell like fireworks, like a lit punk. I remembered sudden heat. I remembered soft carpet and then enclosed warmth and the smell of fresh dirt. I remembered filling out paperwork while wrapped up in half-a-mile of gauze. I remembered a man, a man in a white sweater, wearing a Los Angeles Dodgers hat. I remembered the phrase *unofficial witness protection program.* I also remembered a word, a word attached to a person. A *name.* And yet no face lingered behind these two syllables, this blaring cluster of contrived honesty steeped in some rugged brain cell that opts not to mingle with its billion x billion companions. It's as if its axons and tendrils have been lopped off and, like some humming, aged neon sign, it stubbornly emitted one word into the void:

Dover.

Over and over again: *Dover, Dover, Dover...*

Since there were no trees to climb, Bentley sometimes walked around on all fours. He moved slowly like a sloth, same speed as a live feed from Kinshasa.

He was not on all fours now, though. Right now he was being a good biped and yelling at Maps and me.

"Important guests! Necessary!"

"How long they staying?"

"Indefinitely!"

I had confiscated a cowboy hat from one of the Texans ("Security measures"). I put it on Maps and she made that nauseatingly cute face that everyone makes when they try on a big silly hat: round lips, widened eyes, head cocked… She put it back on my head and said it looks better on me and I concurred so she feigned indignation.

On top of JVS was a paved version of the Bonneville Salt Flats. Everything is white and flat and glistening, and the horizons are terrified of each other. This is the runway. Blinking blue lights pocked its expanse. An enormous zeppelin, the size of four-and-a-half Hindenburgs, was docked on the far crust. Planes are taxied around by muscular robots on wheels. The sunshine is unbearable. No one is up here. Five minutes in these UV rays equates to a weekend of flopping around on a Jamaican beach minus your Coppertone. This is the sun that blisters. This is the sun that makes you want to move to Montreal or Seattle. The wind is rebuffed by anti-wind. Anti-wind is a brigade of fierce nanobots that form an invisible penumbra around the runway. "Utility fog" they called it in the day when people still said words like "Globalization" and "Cyberspace."

A slender Learjet, moored in solitude, expelled its contents into the runway below, impregnating it with nothing beneficial…

"I'm not here to visit," said Mr. Visitor.

"You still need a portpass, sir," said Ms. Maps.

"A portpass? What's wrong with you? *Pass*port. Say it with me…"

Mr. Visitor was not Mr. Visitor. He was Tether Pass, which made his associate Mrs. Visitor, Mary Pass. His other associate, one Pal Iberville, the muscle of the gang, wrapped in the musky tweed of an antebellum attorney, remained cloaked in the precariousness of his birth name.

"I know what a passport is, *sir*," said Ms. Maps. "I need your portpass first. It's different."

"Well, you can't have my portpass because I don't have a goddamned portpass. Never even heard of a goddamned portpass."

"Interesting."

"Sure is, ain't it?"

"Why did you not obtain a portpass?"

Tether Pass grinned and checked his impatience. He did something like a geriatric curtsy and said, "My excuse, Lord, will be to admit that I have no excuse."

"Interesting."

"Still is, no doubt about it."

"What is your business here, Mr. Visitor?"

"I'm here for Doyle. We, as in the one-two-three of us, are here for Doyle."

"Doyle?"

"Badger, I mean."

"Badger? You mean Captain Quartermile?" Maps asked, comprehensively puzzled by the three new guests.

"Yes, that is 1000% correct. We're here for Captain Quartermile," said Mary Pass.

"Surely he is not expecting you."

The three of them looked at each other. "Surely he is not."

"Interesting."

"No, it is no longer interesting. It is dull," said Tether Pass. "Dull, dull, dull!"

Ms. Maps was unequipped to deal with any variety of conflict so she slipped away from her desk and summoned Bentley...

"Which of you is Trant?" This was Bentley. The five of them were in the Inquisiting Lobby, a hyperwhite room streaked with the cartoon brutalism and bubbly poles and pipes of a Bjork video. One of the walls was a television—a television that was tuned to mute static.

"None of us is Trant."

"I was told Weldon Trant from the Fraternal Assembly of Texas Trillionaires was to be arriving on that plane: the one out there with the little blue and red star on it."

"Who told you that?"

"Mr. Trant told me that."

"Incorrect, sir, you're incorrect," said Tether Pass, sharply. "I believe Mr. Trant told you, Mr. Bentley, that he is sending a delegation from his closest ally." Tether Pass put his arms around his companions. "We are that delegation. We are that closest ally."

"You are coming from the U.S., are you not?"

"Technically that statement is correct," said Mary.

"Oh, is that so?" said Bentley, getting visibly flustered.

Tether Pass said, "What Mrs. Visitor here means is we're from the U.S. but it's not the U.S. you're talking about."

"Uncertain Stars, pal," said Mary.

And Pal, playing the Curly of the bunch said: "What? Oh, gotcha."

"The Cyclical Night. Ever hear of it? We're like the Jefferson Starship of the Cyclical Night. And we need Doyle."

"You mean we need Badger," said Mary Pass, who was dressed like a dollar store Barbarella.

"Right."

Bentley, whose patience had long since evaporated, said, "I'd like to talk to Mr. Trant about this."

Weldon Trant was to the world of oil what Howard Hughes was to the world of aviation. The only difference, aside from Hughes's libidinal bravado and Trant's necessary abstinence due to his size (at 7ft, 550 he looked like a man blown up: not exploded, but made larger by way of air pump; he looked like the wobbly thing at sea that contained Armstrong, Aldrin, and Collins), was that while Hughes had coincided with the age of aviation (born two years after Kittyhawk), Trant was doing his business at the tail end of the age of oil. His business? Making oil out of cabbages. Making oil out of *anything*. Nanos again: Tiny robot workers scooting decimal points around, underground, outside of the ubiquitous gaze of mankind, outside of the paranoid brow of 21st century tattletale culture. Federal law had limited nanotechnology to the field of medicine; therefore Trant, also unlike Hughes, was conducting his business illegally. Illegal, however, loses weight in the world of trillionaires. Illegal was made legal, or it was made unseen. It was made never known and never discussed. A million dollar handout when you are in the trillions, when you own every sports team in Texas, when you own three English Premier League teams, one Serbian team (Red Star Belgrade), Peru ("practically"), SeaLand, CNN, NBC, ABC, and every other acronym east of the Rockies—yes, when you've got that kind of money, a million dollar handout, a parcel that arrives in a manila envelope with a little blue and red star in the top left corner, becomes quotidian, reflexive, and plain ol' easy. It becomes "tiny gratuities": something just easier done than not done. It becomes the Parliament Light you give to the bum who holds the door open for you at the 7-11. It becomes the three dimes and a penny you gently set in the guy's guitar case at the top of the Metro. And when you're dealing with the sort of advanced expendability that that kind of money allows, the options for hobbies become exponential. You don't play golf. You don't keep up with the aquarium. You don't do gardening. What you do is you buy teams. And then you buy countries. And then you grow old and begin to worry about your mortality. So you buy medicine—not the item, but the field. But what can that do aside from just suspend? So you buy religion, but that sure as hell isn't any fucking fun, so you buy cults. You buy *a* cult. You buy the one that gives you visible proof of a shot at immortality. You buy the one that goes off and fetches you a Visigoth or a dinosaur egg. It's them you buy, and then you do what? You give them money and you give them power—

—and you give them a Lear jet.

"Trant will tell you the same thing we've told you," Tether Pass said. He handed Bentley a check with assembly line of zeros on it. "This is for you, Mr. Bentley. Our way of saying thank you for your congeniality and your cooperation."

"Wow," said Bentley. "That's very generous."

"Sure, sure," said Mary Pass. "So where is Badger?"

Where was Badger? In my room, under the bed.

"Just come out. I can't talk to you like this," said the static.

"No."

"Pretty please?"

"No, goddamnit. What the hell are you? And why are you in my room? " I asked the strange membrane of TV static that was hovering just above my floor. The Master Blaster was idling just in front of me, a tiny flame danced at the mouth of its cannon.

The static floated closer.

I said, "Don't make me blast you."

The top tips of the static arched in a shrug. "Ain't flammable, friend," it said.

The static formed a television screen, complete with rabbit ears and said, "Just watch this, okay? We don't have much time. Pass is here already, watching his friend Pal beat up on that weirdo boss of yours…. Can't believe they got here before me. Friggin' Asteroid Belt, adds thirty minutes to your commute no matter what time of day it is."

I watched the screen on the static… The pixels conspired to sway back and forth at a slow, hypnotic rhythm. Peering into its colorless murk was like chasing some unseen fish through muddy water… And then time and space fell away from me—and there I am in a room—in an attic, and there's the same static, glowing and hovering, and I'm afraid, I'm tugging at a hatch and I'm terrified… And then I am listening, with a residual caution that is visible, and then I'm smirking and shaking my head… I realized I was doing the latter combo in real time. I was smirking and shaking my head at the screen on the static. And now I am remembering… I am remembering Tether and Mary and Paulo and Tony. I am remembering Dover and a walking cactus. I am remembering Dallas Austin Houston and I am remembering the panic attack from the static in my attic, and I am remembering *Kyle* and Kyle is God or God is Kyle… And then, there, on that impossible television, I am exploding…

"How long?"

"Five years."

"Five years since I killed Houston?"

"Five years and then some. But you didn't kill Houston. They did."

The projector whirred and a 6 x 6 image of the terminal appeared on my wall. Three vertical figures hovered above two horizontal figures.

"The Passes, plus Pal."

I touched the shapes of Maps and Bentley. "What'd they do to them?"

"They're fine. They're asleep. Tether gave them checks—checks with epibatidine mixed in with all those zeros."

"Epiwhat?"

"Epibatidine. It's extracted from the phantasmal poison frog, or *epipedobates tricolor*. It's two hundred times the strength of morphine but completely non-addictive. It's a very handy tranquilizer for the frugal. And it works on contact."

The three vertical figures exited the scene on my wall. Kyle said, "You should leave. Get down to the city and disappear."

"How? You know I've never left this thing."

"Easy. Just jump."

~2~

Decent Descent

Jumping from a platform 100,000 feet above the equator requires a brand new level of faith. It requires a *transcendental* level of faith—or just an adequate level of insanity. Or both. And I had neither.

My glider creaked and I was not okay with this. It creaked and it squeaked and it made other sounds you wouldn't expect a glider to make. A human voice, for example. A human voice that said, "Where to, bub?"

The glider's cockpit was roomy and all glass, which made for good visibility. My head was wing-level, so I could see the stratospheric expanse above and below me. Kyle bubbled in silence on one of the console's many screens. Where to, indeed…

"Can we make it to Rio?" I asked the glider.

"Usted prefiere espanol? Cual Rio?"

"No, no, English, English."

"Ah, lo siento. I mean *sorry.*"

"I'm asking if we can we make it to Rio de Janeiro."

"We can make it *near* Rio de Janeiro."

"How near?"

"I can drop you 22.4 kilometers southwest of the city line."

Hmm. That would have me landing in the mud and flames of the city's crust. I opted for Sao Paolo. Liberdade: the heart of Brazil's Japanese community. The glider assented.

"Can you put me down on the street?

"Too many helicopters. I'm going to have to drop you 2.6 kilometers from your destination. I can put you in a soccer field that's about a half an hour trek from Liberdade," said the Glider. "Biggest city named after a person, you know? Sao Paolo. *Saint Paul.* Second biggest? Not sure, but I'd guess Ho Chi Minh City."

Great. A multilingual glider with a penchant for geography trivia.

"You know, Sao Paolo has more registered helicopters than any other city in the world. Because of all the traffic, I guess, and the kidnappings. Hold tight. I'm putting my landing gear down."

And below me was the city, and its endless glade of dominoes and canines and molars and incisors. And helicopters: dozens of them, zipping above the buildings with menacing self-importance. A ceiling of cloud coverage the color of oatmeal sprawled above me, opaque and invariant.

My nerves tingled and I felt the cool wisp of fear. My subconscious exclaimed: *attention!* Movement in the sky. Above me to the right. And then it was gone: A phantasmal silhouette: The silhouette of a something the size of the glider but with a pair of legs dangling from it.

I knew what I glimpsed was real, and I had the intuitive feeling that it was benign, or, at worst, mired in impartiality. But whatever it was had done evil by allowing itself to be seen. Its presence provided an additional question mark to the crescendo of otherness that had so very recently invaded my life. A host of doubts and fears began to ignite within me, and my memory reacted.

"Al Key."

"Pardon?" said the glider.

"Not you, I'm talking to my weirdo friend here. What was Al Key all about? And that voice of the Metro business?"

Kyle said, "Al Key was—and don't get mad, friend—Al Key was kind of a test. See, you never did anything adventurous or remotely life-risking, and you were way too dadgum cautious at the crosswalks. I'd been trying to get you splattered by a bus for I don't know how long! So I had to drop you in the middle of mass murder to see if you really were immortal. No doubt about it now, though. You're the real deal."

"The real deal, eh? Yeah, lucky for me, otherwise I'd be yesterday's news. Pretty lousy way to go out, too."

"True, true, but I would've definitely put you up in Heaven. Even though technically…"

The mention of Heaven zapped my nervous system optimistically. "Heaven? There really is a Heaven?"

"Yes sir, absolutely there is. I mean, it's not full of people wearing giant gold crowns with jewels all over them, but it's a pretty nice place. Free chips and salsa in every restaurant, and it's socially acceptable to walk around everywhere in your robe and slippers. Also, football season lasts ten months, and there are no mosquitoes or jellyfish or sexually transmitted diseases. Plus, the drinking water doesn't have dookie matter in it like it does where you come from."

So there is a Heaven. Swell news, all that… And then its charcoaled counterpart seeped out of the grates of my noodle. If there's a Heaven then there must be a….

I said to Kyle, "What about Hell?"

"Well, if you go to Hell, it just means you get reincarnated."

"What? That's silly. You get reincarnated and then go to Hell?"

"No, you get reincarnated and come back here."

"So, you don't go to Hell?"

"Yes, you do go to Hell. You *come back* to Hell."

"You're telling me this is Hell? Here?"

"Yes, sir…"

I could feel the glider's descent sharpen in my testicles. The city glowed below.

"So we're in Hell right now? *I'm* in Hell right now?"

"Yes," Kyle said. I sensed he was getting a little tired of my questions. His problem, not mine. I chewed on this Hell-as-reality business for a little bit and was left with a cruddy aftertaste.

I said, "So being immortal essentially means I'm stuck in Hell. What a bum deal, man."

"I guess it does kind of mean that. Never really thought about it."

"You condemned me to Hell just because I'm immortal?"

"You condemned yourself to Hell by gobbling up all that stardust. You were very ambitious in your pre-life, it seems."

"My pre-life?"

"Yes. Before you are born, if you're not being reincarnated, you're a conglomeration of wayward anti-matter, or dark matter, that gains its potential identity by accumulating *matter* matter and replicating and reproducing it. Your matter is stardust. Literally. That's what makes you, well, special. Skyfell 1.0: the Sun before the Sun. A very special star—and the base of your being."

So that's what I'm all about. Animated stardust rendered in snips and snails and puppy dog tails. I got strafed by the spook mumps, that fierce existentialist tremor that can upright the most solidified of psyches. I moseyed back to "normal thoughts" until I was a safe distance. Then I let what Kyle said sink in and said, "Just me? I'm the only immortal?"

"Well, not counting me, of course, there is one other."

We circled the soccer field. The stands were full even though there was seemingly no soccer match taking place. The gaze of the mass of spectators was inverted and animated. It was a tangle of slo-mo mayhem, like a 5am orgy. Cars and jeeps and trucks were docked at the base of the stands, illuminating them with their headlights. I saw glistening motion and pale faces. Something was wrong with these people.

I said, "Who's the other one?"

And Kyle said to the glider, "Not here."

And the glider said, "Where?"

And Kyle said, "Another field."

A sole memory came forth from the murk of my brain, summoned by the scene below. The memory of a somewhat dilapidated anecdote I overheard from one of the many faceless tourists at the Stratoport. The details had long eroded, but the subject and its leftfield grotesqueness remained:

Knife party.

We banked left to the wail of wind resistance and the sodden red jiggle of the stands ebbed from sight.

I went to a French restaurant in the Japanese district of Sao Paulo. The whole place was the color of dark tobacco. The tables and chairs were sturdy and plentiful… Everything wooden, good wood, as it damn well should be in the only country in the world named after a type of wood. Chimerical illumination haunted the walls and tables and chairs: the result of small but ambitious fireplace. Sparse Japanese chatter mingled with sparser French and Portuguese and piano and violin.

I ordered a Dewar's on the rocks and stared at my map.

The glider was gone, spent. It had been designed to escape from the stratoport and nothing more. I felt something like sorrow leaving it there in the field to be gnawed on by salvagers. Kyle disappeared, as he does, to no telling where. In short, I was on my own and I was fine with that. I had money, and lots of it (life in the stratosphere means a pregnant savings account), my passport, and a backpack full of closet and bathroom fundamentals.

My plan was simple: Continue to evade Tether Pass and his gang and go back to where I came from: Washington, DC.

And I did just that, as you'll see shortly. But first, where is my old fling, Dover Datsun? Hell, I've nearly forgotten about her, myself. Here's what we can do: We can go back in time five years and eavesdrop on a cell phone conversation between two peculiar new characters: Whipple Van Ward and Howie Goodge.

"Goodge?"

"Yeah."

"Whipple."

"What can I do for you, Whipple?"

"You in the bathroom or something? Got a hell of an echo."

"No, on a plane. On *your* plane."

"Still?"

"Still."

"She there with you?"

"Yes sir, she is. Picked her up in the Yucatan."

"Good. When you back in Denver?"

"Sooner than later. The little screen's telling me I'm way up at the tip-top of New Mexico now."

"Run into any of Trant's boys?"

"No, I didn't, but they got the other one, as you know."

"I'm not concerned about the other one. Smithereens. Must've not been legit. You test that one yet?"

"Oh, I tested her. I dunked her head in the ocean for ten minutes straight and she comes up calling me an S.O.B. and everything else. She's legit, alright. Either that or God's gift to Polynesian pearl divers."

"Goody gumdrops. My own John Merrick and I don't even have to rent a tux."

"John what?"

"John *who*. John Merrick. The Elephant Man."

"The Elephant Man?"

"In this case, the Elephant *Wo*man. The Elephant Woman and the Invisible Man."

"Who's the Invisible Man?"

"Well, you are."

"Oh, I ain't invisible."

"Then how come I've never seen you?"

"You've seen me plenty of times. Just didn't know it was me. Whatever the case, I'll be seeing *you* pretty darn soon. Pilot wants me to shut up and buckle up."

"Okay, Howie."

"Alright, Whipple."

~3~

New Channels and a Little Big Battle

I had been back a year before anything happened. I had succeeded in maintaining a dull anonymity to my new life back in DC. I didn't travel or do anything that might alert Pass and his gang. I rented a little studio apartment on Massachusetts Avenue, got a job bartending in a Thai restaurant, got another job scooping elephant pooh at the zoo. I didn't really need these jobs, but not working doses you, or, at least, me, with spiritual atrophy and a vague self-loathing. I spent a lot of time in the bookstores, especially in the science and philosophy sections. I dated a couple of gals off and on, went to the movies alone…. There was no sign of Pass, no word from Kyle (although I "prayed" to him every night)…

…And then it all came at once. Things started to unravel one night after a Capitals game. I had gone there with Bela, a Pakistani gal by way of Phoenix that I had sort of been seeing. A dapper chick with enough supplemental quirk to keep me interested. For example, she had a thing for cars. Not in an auto-eroticism sort of way, but rather the car itself. She wouldn't shut up about Cadillacs and how just thinking about one made her giddy.

We were at an Irish bar near the Verizon Center: Four pints of Boddingtons for me, three Jack & Gingers for Bela. We left the place a little drunk. It took a while for us to hail a cab. We must've watched twenty of them roll by that were already occupied. Eventually we took up posts: Bela on the south side of the street and me to the north. Bela nabbed one after about five minutes. The cab smelled of vanilla. Some James Brown song that I'd never heard before was playing on the radio. Bela told the cabbie to take us to 16th and Kalorama. She detected my puzzlement.

"Do you mind if we stop off somewhere?"

"No, that's fine. What's on 16th and Kalorama?"

"A friend's place. It won't take long."

She asked the cabbie to pull into the Dorchester building. The Dorchester was a gigantic and old apartment complex that sprawled along Sixteenth across from Meridian Hill Park. I'd never known anyone that lived there but was still aware of its past celebrity tenants, including one of Marion Barry's hookers/drug suppliers and even, for a brief time, JFK. We paid the cabbie. Bela fumbled through her purse until she produced a magnetic key on a keychain it shared with only one other key. She beeped us through the front door.

"My friend went to Costa Rica for a month and I'm house-sitting for him. Really it just means I have to come over and feed the cats once a day."

"What a pal."

"Not really. He's paying me big bucks to do it."

Bela led me down a long corridor with carpet whose appeal lied only in its absurd and blatant hideousness. The left wall was completely covered by a long mirror. I watched myself as I walked along. I didn't look drunk. I did look tired, though, and my eyes were very red. The Dorchester was terribly quiet and smelled like an old library.

We took the elevator—a very small elevator considering the amount of tenants that must've lived here. Bela pressed the button for the eighth floor. We exited and I followed her through a seemingly labyrinthine hallway. I could smell the residue of the tenants in the rooms as we passed by them: Curry, cigarette smoke, some synthetic floral smell, animals. Bela stopped suddenly at room 802. She used the other key of hers on the door.

"This building can be a little spooky. Thanks for coming with me."

"No problem at all. I actually like walking around buildings I have no business being in. Do you have access to the roof?"

She opened the door and said, "I don't know. Maybe. I've never tried to go up there."

She slid her hand against the wall until she found the light switch. The apartment was a studio, a rather large one, and it was in shambles. The rugs were askew and a CD rack appeared to have toppled over, spilling its contents all across the floor. I was greeted by the sound of broken glass being trod upon—and cats: two of them, meowing hysterically and tangling themselves in my legs with conditional affection. These guys were hungry, or at least they thought they were.

"My God, what have you guys *done?*" Bela said.

I looked down at the cats. One was black and skinny with yellow eyes gleaming in permanent smile. The other was fluffy and grayish—calico they called it, I guess—with a pompous stupid face. I picked up the skinny guy to a motor parade of purring.

"Oh, you little monsters!" Bela kept saying.

The room really was a disaster. Closer inspection revealed the determination of their efforts: a sliding closet door was off a hook, pens were without tops, a fern had been toppled—but not until it was on the recliner, the phone sat off the hook, an LA Galaxy scarf had been singled out for chewing while its neutral brethren hung undisturbed. They'd even opened up his bathroom cabinet and pulled out its contents: several back issues of Playboy sat in crude display across the floor.

"Vindictive little bastards," I said. The cats stared up at me with anticipation. The fluffy guy I didn't like scampered into the kitchen and then turned around to see if I was following him. "Goddamn kitty Mafia, eh?"

I helped Bela with the CD rack. The slathering of CDs suggested they were once in alphabetical order.

"What are their names?"

"Reno and Vegas, though I don't know which is which."

The skinny black fellow joined his buddy in the kitchen. Bela and I wordlessly collected the Playboy magazines and then went about tidying everything up a bit. We put the futon sheets in a pile near the door. Bela said she'd deal with everything else tomorrow. I fed the cats to an earful of desperation. The spoiled little brats still had food in their bowl from the last time Bela had fed them.

We sat down on the couch. Bela turned on the TV and then got up to use the restroom.

"That TV has every channel ever," she said through the bathroom door.

"Every channel ever?"

"I can't imagine there being more. Flip around, there's like five thousand."

I played around with the remote. Channel 545 was showing the Duke throw a punch in slow motion. The mustachioed and dark-skinned recipient of the punch looked increasingly distraught about the situation as the frames slowly progressed. The bottom right side of the screen said JWC. A little blue cowboy hat was perched atop the C.

"John Wayne Channel."

"*What!*"

"Nothing! Talkin' to myself."

"*What!*"

I flipped up one to 546 and was greeted by the horsehead nebula accompanied by some terrible Theremin-heavy ambient music.

I heard the toilet flush and Bela came in and sat down next to me.

"Outer Space Channel. Images from the Hubble, but they're all kind of old."

"Aren't they inherently kind of old?"

Stephan Hawking's voice was pasted on top of the ambient music. He was saying "Eternity" over and over. The Theremin spazzed as more synth-washes accumulated. I expected Carl Sagan to jump in on back-up vocals any time now.

Bela commandeered the remote. It was a non-descript remote, the simple universal variety. Certainly not the behemoth I'd expect from a TV that displayed so many channels.

"Such a small remote for so many channels," I said.

"Really all you need are nine digits and a zero."

Indeed.

Bela found static. "Wait, leave it here," I said.

The static frenzied, but there was no hint of sentience.

"Nevermind. Proceed."

Bela found a channel in the low thousands that was playing an old film noir. Fred MacMurray was throwing a pair of crutches from the back of a moving train. I'd seen this movie before so I knew why he was doing it, but out of context it looked ridiculous. He looked like a man who was really going out of his way to get himself into trouble.

"I'm sleepy," Bela said. "We can just crash here if we want. My friend's bed is the size of a Stingray."

"A stingray? That's not very big."

"Not the animal, the car!"

"Ah, gotcha."

Bela started to drift. I caressed the back of her head and watched Fred MacMurray jump off the back of the train. Within minutes she was as limp as undercooked bacon. I slid out from under her and found a closet with some blankets in it and covered her up.

I contemplated going. And then I contemplated staying. A classic dilemma. I opted to stay. Going would've been more mysterious, more film noir, but also more inconvenient. I checked the fridge for something to drink—preferably something alcoholic. Inside of it were five bottles of some cleverly named microbrew. The bottles were heavily labeled with some purple and orange clip-art featuring some ferocious looking varmint with a buck-toothed smile brandishing a pickaxe. I tried to open one of the beers and then I rummaged around one of the kitchen drawers for a damn bottle opener (did this beer really merit accessories?). The beer tasted like a science experiment with malt and hops and baking soda and vinegar. My dubious taste theory about the apartment's tenant grew stronger. The Utah Jazz magnet on the fridge all but solidified it.

I peeled Bela's fingers from the remote and flipped around a bit. I ended up settling for a replay of an Arsenal/Tottenham match from back in 2004. As a Tottenham fan, this was the equivalent of an Iraqi tank captain watching footage from the first Gulf War. I cursed seven times in six seconds and changed the channel. I tried channel 666, out of curiosity. Ah, the 700 Club Network, of course. Clever, guys. Too bad your fan base isn't. This is the real beginning of the end, Mr. Pat Robertson. Never mind all that business in the book of Revelation. Let's see…Was there a baseball network? Of course there was. But where? Oh, too much! I found the channel with static and pressed the mute button. The fluffy cat jumped up in my lap so I poured some beer on him. Bela stirred silently. I retreated from the couch.

"You in there?" I asked the television. In the back of my head, I realized that I was now thoroughly drunk. However lousy and terribly conceived that last beer was, it had succeeded in putting me over the top.

"Kyle?"

The TV remained silent. I wished I was still at the hockey game. I wished that I could go to hockey games in my robe. I longed for my robe. I longed for *any* robe. I checked the tenant's closet for a robe. Nope, no robes here. I checked his bathroom. A thick fluffy robe the color of cheese grits hung from the back of the door. I took off my clothes, except for my boxers, and tried it on. It was rather large but I liked my robes one size too big anyway. I liked to get lost in my robes.

I stole another science-experiment beer (the way I saw it, I was doing this guy a favor) and then dug around in the closet until I found a pair of flip-flops. I slid Bela's shoes off her feet, gently kissed her forehead, and soundlessly exited the apartment.

The roof, to my surprise, was populated. There were two clusters of people, both situated around lamps: a smaller cluster and a larger cluster. They were at opposite corners of the patio. The larger group emitted some sort of weird bombilation, like they were all talking at the same low frequency, while the smaller group seemed more typical with its conversational fluctuations. It had the ebb of flow of evening anecdote with the occasional assault rifle burst of female laughter. Neither seemed particularly attractive nests of social interaction so I took a spot in a plastic chair in an unpopulated corner. The shadows concealed me fairly well even though I had noticed a few of the people had glanced over at me. Someone somewhere was playing a twelve-string acoustic guitar.

A desert of gravel separated the patio area from the actual ledge of the roof. Miscellaneous pipes and metal contraptions of unknown usage thrust out from the gravel like post-apocalyptic cacti. I counted six planes in the night sky and one helicopter—a lot of buzzing around for a no-fly zone. To the north was the trio of ill-lit cathedrals that sat where Mt. Pleasant, Sixteenth St., and Colombia intersected. The electric skylines of Bethesda and Silver Spring radiated in the distance behind them. To the west was the National Cathedral. It shone white like a magic city from an old children's book. The only other heavyweight building in the area was that Krushchevian juggernaut, 2112, that sat at the base of Meridian Hill Park. Beyond it laid the Capitol and all of its self-importance and clean-cut sentries.

Someone from the small group approached me.

"Hello."

"Hello."

"Nice robe."

"Thanks."

"It looks comfortable."

"It *is* comfortable."

I couldn't tell if the person was a girl or a guy. The voice was androgynous and neutered—or spayed. Not deep, not high, not lispy, not gravelly, it was the voice of a guy pretending to be a girl or a girl pretending to be a guy. A loose black sweater and pair of dark jeans did well to conceal any portending curves or bumps. A mile and a half of scarf hid the presence—or absence—of an Adam's apple. The shadows themselves had taken care of my spotting any facial hair or feminine accessories.

"How is your night going?" he/she asked.

"Not bad. I'm tipsy as shit," I said. "And I can't find my friend."

"Is your friend up here somewhere?"

"I don't think so."

"Where did you last see your friend?"

"I last saw him in a talking glider above Sao Paulo."

The visitor's face lit up in the shadows. This seems to have been the best possible answer. I looked up at him/her. The hair was cut short and choppy. The wind kept the left side of it permanently vertical. His/her features reminded me one of the Vulcan women on Star Trek, but stricken with a dose of tepidity that slackened them enough to lose any trace of sci-fi weirdness. This person was very attractive, either exotically beautiful or uniquely handsome.

"Your scarf,' I said, nabbing one of its tentacles out of the air. "What is it made out of?"

He/she looked down at it. "I'm not sure. Polyester?"

I pulled on the scarf loosely with one hand and soundlessly rubbed my fingernail against it. "No, it's not polyester. It's nice, though, whatever it is."

"Thank you."

I took a sip of beer and winced. The wind had sobered me up a little bit. My visitor took out a pack of Parliament Light Menthols and lit one. A blast of menthol swept into my nostrils. It was a nostalgic smell. It reminded me of days I couldn't possibly relive, days of endearing discomfort and jejune mayhem.

"Would you like to know what the world's worst beer tastes like?" I asked.

Even the laugh was androgynous. "Are you providing me with the opportunity to find out?"

"Yes, I am."

The visitor rubbed the back of his/her head and further mussed his/her hair. "I think I'd rather you describe it."

"I can do that."

He/she sat down.

"Do you know anything about Venus?" I asked.

"Venus the goddess or Venus the planet?"

"Venus the planet."

"I don't really know much about Venus the planet. I do know it's the brightest body in the sky—besides the sun and moon. And I know it's very, very hot."

"That's right. Venus is very hot. Extremely hot. It's hotter on Venus than it is on Mercury—and Mercury is twice as close to the sun."

"Do you know why?"

"I wouldn't have brought this Venus business up if I didn't," I said. "I want a smoke. Do I want a smoke? I don't want a smoke."

"You can have a smoke."

"No, thanks, I'm good. Anyway, Venus is basically one giant mega-Greenhouse effect. It has an extremely dense atmosphere of carbon dioxide. And above this atmosphere roam these clouds made of sulfur dioxide. The smell of burning sulfur? That's sulfur dioxide: a truly rotten chemical compound. Now, imagine if you were to bottle some of this stuff and sell it under the name—" I held up the bottle, "Punxsutawney Phil's Early Spring Ale."

He/she took the bottle and took a sip from it and made a terrible face.

"Oh, God."

"Fucking nightmare, right?"

"It's like liquid burnt pizza. Liquid burnt meat lover's pizza."

"Wow," I said. "That's actually a super accurate description."

He/she took the bottle and read the label. "Where is Strong Arm Tactics Brewery?"

"I'm guessing Pennsylvania."

"You're right," he/she continued reading. "Punxsutawney, Pennsylvania."

A strange high-pitched beeping sound nabbed my attention. It was coming from me; or rather it was coming from one of the robe's pockets. It was my phone. Someone had sent me a message.

Where r you?

It was Bela. My androgynous new friend saw his/her cue. "I'm gonna go steal us a couple of glasses of wine."

I replied to Bela's text message. *Still here. Making friends about a hundred feet above you. Join me?*

My new friend returned with two glasses of white wine.

"I'm not keeping you from your friends, am I?" I asked.

"No, no, you're actually doing me a big favor by providing me with an excuse to get away from them," he/she said, lighting another menthol. "They won't shut up about serial killers. Really I'm just here for their booze."

"Serial killers? What are they, a bunch of criminologists?"

"That's exactly what they are—or what they will be if they ever get out of school."

"Do you always roll with criminologists?"

"Ordinarily, no."

"Are you a criminologist?"

"Oh, God no. I would rather hang out with criminals any day than people who study them," He/she motioned at the group. "I just know a couple of them. Friends of an ex."

"An ex—?"

"Yeah, an ex."

I reluctantly abandoned this talk of his/her ex and said: "Well, you'll be pleased to know I have zero interest in serial killers. To be honest, I could never figure out why they'd want to concern themselves with *people* so much."

"That's exactly—"

"Shhh... Let's not let them infect our conversation."

"Yes, you're right."

We sat quietly. My new friend reminded me of someone, though I couldn't pinpoint who or why. The guy with the twelve-string in the other group, the larger group was actually pretty good. He was playing some delicate tango number. A couple of the women were dancing. Their moves were way too melodramatic for the subtle jangle of the man's guitar. They reeked of contrived sexiness and implied spotlights. They also reeked of weed and patchouli.

"I'm Javelin," my new friend said. "Javelin Till." We shook hands across the table.

"I'm Badger."

"Badger?"

"Yeah, like the varmint."

My pocket beeped again. *En route. How do I get up there?*

"Sorry," I said to Javelin while pressing buttons on my phone. "A friend of mine is joining us, but she can't seem to locate the roof."

I replied to Bela: *Walk up the stairs until you see sky, then just follow the fake coconuts. I'm underneath the fake palm tree. Just next to the koi pond.*

"Your friend found you, eh?"

"Different friend."

"Ah."

I still had zero idea what gender this Javelin was. He/she would do something ambiguously masculine and quickly counter it with some subtle feminine motion.

"Javelin. You know you're the first person I've ever met that was named after a weapon."

A look of mild disappointment overtook Javelin.

"That's what everyone says. Then I remind them they've probably met a Lance before."

I thought about this. I had indeed met a number of Lances.

"You're right. I've known some Lances," I said. "Regardless, Javelin is a far superior name."

"Thank you."

"Are your brothers and sisters named after weapons?"

"I don't have any brothers or sisters. I'm an only child," Javelin said with an air of pouty triumph.

I thought about this carefully. "So, your family consists of a mother and a father and…"

"And me. Just me, my mom, and my dad."

My phone beeped. *I DON'T SEE ANY FAKE COCONUTS!!!!*

"My friend's being a goober. I'm gonna go nab her real quick."

"Sure, sure."

I walked around to the entrance of the roof. Bela was there. She looked tense.

"I'm mad at you," she said. This phrase usually indicated that the person who said it was not really mad at you. "You disappeared and I hate being alone in that apartment. Why are you in a robe?"

"Why are you *not* in a robe? Hey, look, I'm sorry. I was restless and I felt like ambling. I didn't want to bother you because you were out like a British heavyweight," I said. Her scruples were still on all fours, though, and my wisecracks puzzled her further. "Come here, I want to introduce you to my new friend."

Javelin was leaning languidly against one of the large pipes that jutted from the roof.

"Javelin, this is Bela. Bela, this is Javelin."

They shook hands. Javelin offered to get Bela a glass of wine but she declined. Bela had a mug of something. Green tea, it smelled like.

"I've seen you before," Javelin said to Bela. "You're a friend of Diego's, eh?"

"Yes, I am. I'm actually watching his apartment for him here. He's in 802."

"Ah, nice," said Javelin. "He's in Costa Rica, right?"

"Yeah, Costa Rica. Have we met before?" asked Bela. "You look very familiar."

"Maybe. Probably," said Javelin. "You look familiar, too. Maybe you've seen me with Diego. Or I've seen you with Diego."

Diego, Diego, Diego. I felt a tingle of bareback animosity every time I heard the name Diego. What a weird thing to do, actively dislike someone you've never ever met. And what a deliciously easy thing to do, too.

"What's Diego doing in Costa Rica?" asked Javelin.

"He went there to work on his Spanish," Bela said. "He's in some kind of program that guarantees fluency."

Great. A Diego that doesn't even speak Spanish.

I listened to Bela and Javelin talk about this stupid Diego for nearly ten minutes. Where he'd been, what he was doing, how his friends were doing, his family, his job. Bela's green tea seemed to fumigate the whole rooftop. I looked into my glass of wine for solace but the thing had forsaken me. In fact, it seemed set on conspiring against me. I was tired and I wanted to sleep. I breathed a few words like "tired" and "exhausted" until Bela noticed my discomfort. We said goodbye to our androgynous new friend and then stumbled back in the direction of room 802. Soundless lightening played in the far sky. Someone on the roof was taking pictures of it.

"Mr. Pass?"

"Hold, please."

"   "

"Mr. Pass?"

"Speaking."

"This is 3."

"Mmhmm?"

"Uh, the owls are indeed what they seem."

"That so."

"The Dorchester on 16th and Kalorama. Apartment 802."

"He alone?"

"No, he has a female companion with him."

"Good work, 3. Got that shiny nickel waiting for you."

I woke up to the sound of purring. The slim black cat was nestled between Bela and me. He was smiling like he'd just heard a kinda-funny joke. Bela spazzed as if spooked in a dream and rolled over towards me. Her knee poked me in my thigh and I inched away.

What time was it? This Diego hadn't put a clock anywhere in his studio—at least not a luminous clock. Cornflower blue hinted at the crevices in the blinds. It must've been early in the morning. To my surprise my head didn't hurt at all. I did feel heavy and spent, though, and knew there was little chance of getting off this futon anytime soon. I rolled over and fell back asleep.

In my dream there were six of me. The backdrop was Baltimore, but a Baltimore that was huddled and dismal and dark and damp. The lamps were bent and the pathways were tangled and locally silent, although some distant, implied event gave the city a hurried air, and bestowed it with the spooky camaraderie of a tornado shelter or city under siege.

The first me was reading atop a pile of weathered hardcovers. He had a soft, neutered look to him; a pathetic innocuousness, thin-lipped and without humor; a milquetoast mired in the elsewhere of his endless texts. The second me was walking fast, rigid with agenda; an indiscriminate zeal in his confident, sporty focus. His hair was parted and slicked back neatly; his clothes were prep-school and he smelled of Armani Emporium. The third me was steeped in a giant recliner, flaccid with melancholy. His jeans were ripped and his shoes had big holes in them. "My feet are wet," he kept saying. "And I'm out of vitamins, and the *S* key on my computer is screwy, and my bookshelf is wobbly..." His stream of soft-core setbacks was appalling and I wanted to knock him out of his chair and kick him in the gut and give something to really fret about. The fourth me was, well, *me*: familiar and seemingly complete, but suspicious of my presence. "What are you doing here?" he asked and I asked the same of him. We declined to answer each other. Mutually and mildly annoyed, we both backed away and then avoided each other like two guys at a house party wearing the same shirt. The fifth me was the most curious—and the most revolting. He was ghoulish and stricken with a severe slouch—not the geriatric variety but a nearly animalistic slouch. His robe was tattered and pocked with foodstuff. He prowled around in search of some unseen prey, mumbling and slobbering; his arm disappeared into his robe and his hand tugged on his penis erratically. He smoked his cigarette with the determination of someone about to storm a machine gun bunker—puffing frenetically, with exaggerated exhales. He sniffed at me and then continued his crooked scurry. Relief enveloped me when he rounded the corner and was out of sight.

I entered a neighborhood of leaning row houses. The street narrowed and a mist was descended. Water was near, although I could not see it. Steam rose from vents in the pavement. I approached an intersection. A pub was nestled on the corner—its neon lights amplified by the mist. I walked inside and the few faceless heads at the bar swiveled in my direction. The bar was cramped and predominantly wooden. A boxy little television was perched on top of the cigarette machine. Gritty blues petered out of an unseen speaker. There was no sign of a bartender or any other employee. And then I encountered the sixth me: on the television—and on a futon, sleeping. The angle was from above. Bela was next to me, motionless with deep sleep. The view panned out. The Dorchester, the Dorchester and Meridian Hill Park… It continued panning out until I could see the entirety of the stretch of 16th between the U Street Corridor and Mt. Pleasant… And then motion: a taxi cab. The unseen camera zoomed back in. The cab pulled into the front of the Dorchester. The back door of the cab opened and a young boy got out. He looked to be about six or seven; his hair was blonde and styled with Sunday school mousse. He was wearing beige slacks and a white button up shirt. He looked like a tiny politician. The cabby handed the little guy his change and drove off. The boy buzzed himself in and walked down the long hallway toward the elevator. He had a pounce in his gait that was beyond his years. He ignored the old lady at the front desk and pressed the *up* button. He entered the elevator and pressed 8. It was then that I got a look at his face. It was a face with the wrinkled glare of someone six times older, with intelligent grey eyes that were cold and humorless—the eyes of a film noir detective or a Stasi interrogator. I realized that this "little boy" represented everything that was terrible and wretched and unwanted. And then the screen abruptly turned to static—static that said, "Everett, wake up! Run! Now!"

I woke up, thoroughly distressed. I poured the cat's water on Bela's head. She sprung up, confused and terrified. I helped her to her feet and told her we had to leave *now*. She was dazed and upset, but the sincerity of my intensity quelled any resistance from her. *Fire*, she was probably loosely thinking, or *intruder*.

Robed and barefoot, I threw on only my pants on our way out. We entered the hallway.

The little boy from my dream was at the far end of it.

He saw us and began sprinting toward us. We turned and ran toward the exit sign. We banged the door open and double-stepped it down the stairwell. I heard the door bang open again: the little boy was one story above us, his footsteps clacking and echoing in the stairwell.

We reached the basement and ran out into the hallway: a lady with laundry—exiting an elevator. We ran past her into the elevator and I pressed the top button. A bang and more clacking in the hallway—the kid was running toward the elevator….I held my leg up, toes curled back….

I zeroed the kid in the nose with my foot as soon as he came into view. There was a squishy crunch and he fell back as the door closed. The image of that half-second would never leave my memory. *Teeth*—small, pointy, and plentiful—conspiring to create a terrible smile on a sweaty little red face.

We were ascending. I asked Bela if she had her phone. Neither of us had our phones. I told her the kid wasn't a kid and that it had probably been sent to me by my enemies. She asked who my enemies were and I told her she was safe as long as she stayed away from me for a little while. The eighth floor was approaching. Phones or the roof? Phones meant police, but did we close the door? And if we closed it, did we lock it? Did we have the keys? No time to check…

The roof was empty. A garbage can overflowing; some beer bottles moored at its base. The lobby below was on the south side of the building. The Washington Monument was to my left. I picked up the garbage can and ran over to the south side of the roof and began throwing beer bottles overboard.

Bela watched as I tumped the whole can over and bottles and half-eaten burgers and hot dogs and bananas and miscellaneous bags and wrappers disappeared into the night sky. A fusillade of splats and tiny explosions echoed off the buildings around us.

We hid behind the cactus before we realized we were hiding behind a cactus.

"Careful you don't get stuck," the cactus said.

Bela and I yelped simultaneously in double digit octaves.

"Christ. That you?" I asked the cactus.

"Yeah, that me."

"Why are you here? *How* are you here?"

Mr. Catbirddog remained completely still. His blue Nikes barely poked out of the bottom of his cactus suit.

"Here for Goodge, chief. I'm gonna give that little shit a free piggyback ride all the way to Texas."

"Goodge?"

"Howie Goodge. One of Whipple's boys."

"Whipple?"

"Whipple Van Ward: Televangelist and billionaire ten times over. Weldon Trant's #1 enemy. Goodge is on Whipple's payroll, head of the rubber gloves department if you know what I mean. Now, Trant put up a big, big, big bounty on Goodge, and I been hiding out keeping an eye on you waiting for that little bastard to come around chasing you." The cactus bent around and took a look at me. "How you been, Badger? Security gig didn't work out for you, eh? Houston went kaboom before you could even punch in."

"It was a setup."

"Shhh…"

About fifteen feet away the door opened and the little boy emerged. He had what looked like a pair of hair clippers in his hand—a tazer, that I had not noticed earlier. He spotted us immediately and charged.

For the second time in five minutes, the little boy got a full-force foot in the face—this time by way of Catbirddog's Nikes. Goodge went momentarily airborne and then lay sprawled on in the pool of gravel. Catbirddog pounced and inside of a second he had Goodge over his shoulder and bound and gagged with duct tape.

"Decoy gets 2%. I'll send ya'll a check."

A tubby lady emerged out of nowhere. She was head-to-toe in rent-a-cop charcoal—the security guard, no doubt, that I had summoned by tossing over all that garbage.

"What are you people doing up here?" she said.

Catbirddog flashed her a badge and said, "Lieutenant Catbirddog with the PCPLSDMDMA."

"The *hunh*?"

"I'm gonna need to commandeer your flashlight."

He took her flashlight and thwacked Goodge on the head. "Rabid coon got a hold of him," Catbirddog said before the security guard could protest. "Better off unconscious till I can get him the antidote."

"Rabid coon? There ain't no rabid coons up here."

"Not anymore, there's not. Whole bunch of 'em just went over the side in a garbage can… Hell, they're probably halfway to the White House by now. Mean little bastards. No tellin' what they got planned."

Security guards, like writers and massage therapists and restaurant managers, generally end up doing what they do because of a lack of qualification in other arenas. They're ill-equipped for life, much less any sort of vocation in that life, and, worse, they know it, so they do what they do, or try to do what they do, until their liver or lungs or both finally give way to the peace and quiet they've longed aspired to attain. I had no idea whether Catbirddog had read *The Art of War*, but nevertheless he knew to go outside the realm of his enemy's experience—and in this case, his enemy's experience was slim. The Cactus suit/gagged boy/rabid coon trio was more than sufficient to immobilize the rent-a-cop and her faculties.

As he walked past her with Goodge over his shoulder, Catbirddog said to us, "Text me so I can get your address! My name spells my number. Uncanny as hell, didn't even mean for it… Like *divine intervention* or somethin'."

The security guard said to us, "That your tazer?"

"Nope," I said, elbowing in the direction of the door closing behind Catbirddog. "Must be his."

"Where's he taking that boy?"

"Hospital, I guess."

The security guard looked at me, still in Diego's robe, my pants poking out at the bottom, and then at Bela, and then back at me. "Ya'll some weird people."

We all stared at the tazer until I picked it up. It was bigger than the tazers I had seen on TV, and deceivingly heavy. "Thing's larger than life. My life, at least."

"Mine, too," the security guard said.

I turned and looked at her. "We're going to leave now. If you do have to report this, then I suggest you tell everything just as it happened. Don't leave out any details, okay?"

"Okay."

"You take care."

"Okay, you too."

Bela and I went to 802 and gathered our things. Then we went downstairs and walked outside to the street. She kissed me on the cheek and told me that she'd call me tomorrow, and then the S2 bus came by and scooped her up. She waved to me as the bus sped off. I waved back and accidentally hailed a cab.

~4~

Queer Fortune, Javelin's Jobs, and the Moose House

The next few weeks provided me with nothing more than a severe dose of ennui. Each day fizzled into the next and I can scarcely produce a solid memory of anything involving laugher or excitement. Sharks were all over the news again, which generally meant that humans were getting along relatively okay with each other. I discovered online shopping and emptied half of my account with the zeal of a conquistador. It all started with a pair of jogging shoes, and this led to jogging accessories which neatly sequed into soccer paraphernalia. CDs and books were thrown into the mix on whim. I bought a Greek fishermen's hat supposedly made from actual Greek fishermen. I even bought a cat online, which I had no idea you could do—the quintessential way, I thought, for me to celebrate the first decade of the twenty-first century. The spree culminated with an actual-size wall poster of former Tottenham forward Robbie Keane which routinely catches me unawares and scares the living hell out of me.

Bela and I talked to each other on the phone a couple of times. Whatever intimacy we'd developed over the last few weeks had been replaced by this asexual-voice bandying about nothing in particular. The calls always ended in a forced encore of a flutter of ideas of when and where we should meet again. Then we switched to emailing and texting, usually for the sake of clarifying when we would talk on the phone next. In short, meta-communication had claimed two more victims. I never saw her again.

One afternoon I found myself in a particularly existential mood. A combination of the right elements (sleep deprivation, hangover, hunger, and crisp weather) had rendered everything fragile, surreal, and a little frightening. I put on my Greek fisherman's hat, pulled it low to hide from the world, and took the Metro up to Van Ness just to see if other parts of the city did indeed still exist. I stopped off at a Chinese restaurant which had posted accolades about its Peking duck on just about every vacancy on its walls. I ordered a cup of hot and sour soup and some shrimp fried rice from a good-natured, corpulent waitress. Some crustaceans were huddled together it out in a twenty-gallon tank. They looked resigned and forlorn and I caught myself almost feeling sorry for them.

I ate my dinner with prodigious speed and then scribbled in the air to indicate that I wanted my check. The waitress dropped it off on a little tray. A fortune cookie sat inert next to it. I left thirteen dollars under two quarters and opened up the fortune cookie.

I expected the usual ill-imagined grammatical misfit of miniature praise or aphoristic humdrum. What I found inside could not have been more polar from these expectations. At first I noticed the text: small and plentiful. And then I noticed the words composed of it. And then I must have yelped aloud,

Badger,

Your solar soul mate can be found in familiar dimensions 4am, channel 208

- Confucius

P.S. Where'd you score that hat, the Eastern Bloc or the Great Depression?

I stood up, loud and fast. The waitress had gone into the kitchen. I was alone except for a couple of portly businessmen from New York at a nearby table—their heavily accented gossip had been fumigating the dining room for the entirety of my dinner. They took notice of my panicked state but continued about their business, each sprawling regally, catty-cornered, legs crossed effeminately, their elbows tucked up behind them, hands clasped just southwest of the heart: the typical posture of New York affluence.

The waitress came back out with a basket of rolled silverware. I asked her where she got the fortune cookie. She led me to a pail of fortune cookies and offered me another one, her face wild with worriment. I declined and ran outside. The sun was nestled behind thick clouds but I still formed a visor with my hand. I surveyed Connecticut Avenue, north and then south. I had no idea who or what I was looking for and I saw nothing that was in any way suspicious. I took off running. I ran north, uphill and then downhill. I had been jogging lately, at least once a week. It wasn't going to pay off today. I stopped and looked around again:

There: A man's head, looking at me looking at it, inside a pool of plastic balls at a Burger King playground across the way. I bolted across the street, a car honked, another one swerved. The head smiled, and then it disappeared into the plastic balls. The head was wearing a hat—a Dodgers hat. I ran inside the Burger King and into the playground area. No one was there. I jumped in the plastic balls and dug around maniacally. Someone came in, a plump lady in a Burger King uniform. She asked me to leave, which was fine since I was doing that anyway.

I took the Metro back to Dupont Circle. I ambled up Connecticut Avenue, with no destination in mind. It was 3pm. All the restaurants and bistros and cafes were mostly empty. I took a right on Florida Avenue. I had decided to stick to states and lay off numbers and letters—at least until Florida Avenue turned in the U Street. I looked around dreamily as I walked. The sun was now concealed behind a lone dark cloud. I took a left on 16th Street and walked up a ways. On my left was the big and boxy Dorchester. On my right was Meridian Hill Park. I stopped and stared at the Dorchester's roof. What was Catbirddog up to right now? And what had Trant done with this Goodge fellow? And who the hell was that in the playground in the Dodgers hat? This kind of thinking could rain a lagoon of question marks.

I curbed the internal bandy-fest and walked into Meridian Hill Park.

Meridian Hill Park, or Malcolm X Park, as it's still known in some parts of DC, is stretched across a hill on the north side of the central DC. It's a sizeable oasis of greenery streaked with stone footpaths draped by magnolia trees and man-sized elephant ears. There are a number of Italian-renaissance-style fountains and a large and very long thirteen-basin cascade fountain bisects the southern half of the park. There are statues, too, and they are dreadful. Joan of Arc, for some reason atop a horse, is elfin and sea green. She's riding the horse like it's an electric bull, with her legs and right arm flailing in the air. Dante is gigantic and dark and terrifying. If you squint he could pass for King Kong. The park's drug haven/prostitution days are over, but the stigma has not yet subsided. Consequently the park is still ill-populated.

Atop the park where it plateaus, there are two large fields that are primarily used for soccer, the occasional game of Ultimate Frisbee withstanding. I took a seat on one of the many benches that flanked the fields. The soccer players were in full effect. I estimated that they represented about six or seven different nations. There were three youngsters from probably the Ivory Coast or Senegal, a Jamaican keeper, a duo of Moroccans or Algerians, a lone Brit, a gaggle of probably Mexicans or Salvadorans, and a few Ethiopians or Eritreans. For the life or me, I couldn't figure out how they knew who was on their team and who wasn't.

"Where's your robe?"

Javelin sat down next to me. He/she was wearing a Barcelona jersey over a navy thermal top and grey cargo pants. I caught a whiff of what I swear smelled like CK1.

"You again," I said. "How's life?"

"Better than the alternative? Perpetual? I don't know," Javelin said. I never really wanted an answer when I asked this reflexive as all hell question, alas everyone these days is a goddamn dollar store Oscar Wilde. "You come here to play?" Javelin motioned toward the guys playing soccer.

"No way. Strictly observer. I haven't kicked anything in probably twenty years," I said, omitting the exception of Howie Goodge. "Why, are you going to play?"

"No, I just like to watch. Especially this gang. A couple of them are really good. Keep your eye on the guy in yellow."

I had been watching him and I had realized he was leagues better than the others.

"He's good, for sure. If not a little selfish."

"Nothing wrong with that."

The Jamaican let out of flurry of indecipherable orders to one of the defenders, a young Salvadoran wearing a Boca Juniors jersey. The guy in yellow juked Boca Juniors with ease and sailed a shot over the goalpost. The Jamaican started grumbling and jogged off after the ball.

Javelin turned to me. "Do you live around here?"

"No, I'm down in Dupont. I've got a little studio apartment on Mass Ave, near the Gandhi statue."

"Ah, the building next to the Cosmos Club?"

"That's right."

"I have a friend that lives there. He lives on the fourth floor, I think. 414"

"I'm on the sixth. 614, actually."

"I've been there before. It's nice. At least nicer than the Dorchester."

I shrugged in mild disagreement. "It's an okay place to live, I guess. Heat works, AC works. Garbage chute never clogs up."

Javelin offered me a Parliament Light Menthol and I declined. A new batch of soccer players began to accumulate on the sidelines. They kicked the ball around and feigned impatience. The Jamaican was still grumbling to no one in particular.

"So what's on your agenda today?" I asked Javelin.

Javelin pulled a long drag from his/her cigarette and exhaled with much sound. He/she shut his/her eyes so I took the opportunity to spy for any curves or lumps that might indicate gender—to no avail. There was nothing noticeably present nor absent. Javelin really was androgyny personified.

"Not much," he/she said. "I have to work in a little while."

"What a drag."

"Not really. I dig my job."

"Yeah, you're one of very few."

"The story of my life."

I watched a young woman with a giant stupid-looking dog walk through the congregation of fresh soccer players. A couple of them whistled at her. She ignored them and stared at her dog's rear end as he trotted before her. To her dismay, the big dog walked over to the edge of the grass and laid a mound of turd. She bent over to scoop up the big mound and was barraged by a series of catcalls.

"So what do you do exactly?"

"I don't think I should tell you."

"What a tease."

"That's life."

The soccer players exchanged haphazard and obligatory looking handshakes and then began to disperse. The fresh players moseyed onto the field. Meanwhile, the lady and her jackass dog continued to make enemies. The dog apparently got sight of a squirrel that ran up a tree and began to make a big ruckus about it. The lady held onto the dog's leash with the desperation of an aged angler pulling in a king-sized marlin. The squirrel overhead began squawking and spazzing his tail in an effort to warn his comrades.

"You don't have to tell me. I can find out pretty easily on my own."

"Oh, yeah?"

"I tend bar down in Dupont, and one of my regulars is a bigwig in the FBI. This guy's a total lush. Steady diet of Key Lime Martinis, seven days a week. I have to cut him off night after night. Maybe next time I won't. Maybe next time I'll give him a jumbo shot of Jameson and an index card instead—an index card with the words 'Javelin Till' and 'occupation' on it."

"Ha. It's almost worth me not telling you to see if you could actually pull that off."

"Oh, I could. Easy cheese."

I watched the soccer players begin to run around. Their movements looked chaotic and unnecessary. I didn't understand what they were doing at all. The soccer ball sat inert under a bench.

"I actually have two jobs. One is part-time, the other is full-time. Today I am going to the part-time job. The full time job I never leave. It's always there. It never goes away."

"You're a... I mean, you have a kid?"

"No. No kids. Your Bureau buddy could probably tell you about my part time job. The full time job, however, is above and below every radar on the planet, so don't bother asking me or anyone else about it."

"Seed thoroughly planted. Now I *have* to know."

"Tough stuff, mister."

The soccer players continued to joust and run around erratically. Some of them were standing still, frozen and statue-like. To my astonishment, it occurred to me that the soccer players weren't playing soccer at all—they were playing *freeze tag*. I almost said something to Javelin about it, but an icy air had developed around us, prohibiting any ecto-topical talk.

The soccer players started playing soccer again. I felt a tiny existentialist tingle when I realized I could very possibly go the rest of my life without witnessing another game of freeze tag.

The icy air subsided a bit so I said, "So your part time job is fair game?"

Javelin turned and looked at me. "You really want to know, don't you?"

Not anymore, I didn't. In fact, his/her contrived secrecy was beginning to irritate me. I shrugged again: my default gesture around this strange creature.

"I'm what you'd call a 'vacancy expeditor'," he/she said. "That's how I make money part-time."

"And what exactly does a vacancy expeditor do?"

"Well, there are all sorts of ways to expedite vacancy, but I've found that the most efficient way to, well, get someone to vacate whatever you want vacated, is to haunt them," Javelin said. "I haunt houses for a living."

"You haunt houses. You're a house haunter."

"Yes. I get paid to prompt people to move out of their house or apartment by making them too afraid to live there."

I made a face that exclaimed *how* or *why*.

Javelin explained the whole gig to me, rapidly and with an explosion of gesticulation. Javelin would pause until I nodded and he/she'd continue with this grand screed of the world of house-haunting. Amidst this barrage, I figured it out who Javelin reminded me of: Julia, a boyish nymph of an ex-girlfriend from a loose decade ago. Julia who I called Julie, mistakenly and excessively. Julia who I cheated on, clandestinely and with sound purpose. In the end, I drew ire from my actions. Not from Julia (I have no reason to believe that she ever found out) but from the gossip mongers that stood around in the periphery of that relationship. In their eyes, I was a paradigm of immorality, shredding the fabric of blind constancy, causing harm only to *them*—each who clung to some ephemeral stand-in for true love or whatever they supposed it to be. I had suggested you can indeed live a single life while in a relationship and I had watched their supposed liberal lifestyles morph into the tight-browed and pinched-faced rigor of their parents. I knew nothing of the whole lot of them now, nor did I care to know.

I tuned back into Javelin as he/she finished with a sweeping gesture that implied the need for a *wow* or something like that from me.

"Wow."

"I guess my part time job is rather unusual."

"It's unusual, alright. Wouldn't it be easier if you just sat outside their window and rattled a chain?"

"No, no, too obvious, too fictional, too trite. It's all psychology. You wouldn't believe the research that goes into one target."

"I don't guess I would."

"For example, today I'll be playing the part of a Mrs. X's dead husband. I'm sending her a love letter from him—from the afterlife."

"Won't she notice that it was postmarked from DC?"

"She will not. With any luck, though, she will notice that it was postmarked from Cambodia, the place where he died."

"That's a little cruel."

"It's *a lot* cruel. But maybe you've noticed so is nature."

Sure, sure. Everyone was always using nature as an excuse. Kudzu steals all the light from the white oak, a wasp lays its eggs in a dead tarantula. If that means I can cheat on my taxes and swap price tags at the Goodwill, so be it. People forget, though: Nature is tricky. It doesn't end at the timberline. Landmines and uranium ultimately come from the same star dust as bee spit and Echinacea leaves—that is, if you believe what everyone else believes, or what they go against believing.

"What about the handwriting?" I asked.

"Identical. The terms of endearment? Identical and used sparingly—exact usage as her husband."

"A letter's going to make her move out?"

Javelin lit another menthol. "The letter is phase one. Phase two is a little more gruesome: the pixels on her television will unite to form her dead husband's face. Days later they'll unite again—to form a maggot-eaten skull. And then the phone calls will come: transmissions from her husband's desperate pleas for reinforcements, unanswered pleas that resulted in him getting strung up and skinned like a buck."

Javelin's words prompted disbelief more than disapproval of what he or she was doing. The whole thing seemed to fictional and ridiculous to spur any sour emotions. At last I said, "You've got it all figured out, huh?"

"It's what I do."

"Well, I'd like to wish you good luck but, Christ, what a thoroughly shitty thing to do to someone."

"Perhaps you'd think differently if you knew why my target is being expedited."

I shrugged and stifled a yawn.

"Cat killer. My target poisons her neighbor's cats."

In my opinion this was the only crime worthy of the death sentence. Each of my heartstrings had a dead pussycat hanging from it. I would be infinitely more grief-stricken from spotting a mangled tabby on the side of the road than from reading all the obituaries in the world. And I'd be lying if I said I cried more when my aunt Gretchen died than I did when little Captain Freeway got tangled in my dad's Jeep Wrangler's engine belt. In short, I had a soft spot for cats.

I shared my disdain of cat killers with Javelin through gritted teeth and then asked, "Why didn't they just call the cops?"

"We're quicker and cheaper than dealing with law enforcement and attorneys."

"Amazing. How'd you land this job?"

"I applied for it."

"No kidding?"

"No kidding."

All this cat talk reminded me that I should probably go feed mine.

"I have to get going," I said, standing up. "Glad I bumped into you. And best of luck with the cat killer."

"Thanks. She'll be in Cambodia before the end of the month—if not sooner." Javelin stood up and flicked his/her menthol. "I'll see you around, mister. Ciao."

I walked back out onto Sixteenth Street and hailed a cab.

"Good weather," said the cabbie.

"Very nice day, for sure."

"Is this the same thing? I do not believe so. You see, it is very possible to have a bad day when the weather is nice—and it is very possible to have a nice day when the weather is bad."

I had forgotten: all the cabbies in this city were turning into amateur philosophers. I zipped my lips and stared out the window. My thoughts were clipped and spastic. They jumped from Javelin to soccer to the message in the fortune cookie to the head with the Dodgers hat in the Burger King playground and back. Finally, just after wondering why only baseball coaches were the only coaches in professional sports to still wear uniforms, my thoughts settled on good ol' Brezhnev.

"Mr. Pass?"

"Go 'head."

"Uh, I know where the blue roses grow."

"You do, do ya?"

"2014 Massachusetts Avenue. Apartment 614."

"Good job, 3. Better get yourself a bigger piggy bank."

I cabbed it back to my apartment. I sat on my balcony for a while, sipping Dos XX and listening to old Britpop in my headphones. The sun, seemingly content with exclusively being in this hemisphere today, finally gave way to its fate and submerged in the horizon. I went inside and turned on the TV and muted the volume. I played around on my laptop for a while. I did a web search for Javelin Till. Nothing turned up so I tried variations of the name and nicknames that potentially could have been wrung out of it. Nothing, nothing, nothing. And a search for "vacancy expeditor" produced even more nothing. I called Bela and left a message for her to call me back. I texted her too, but she did not respond. I lied down on my couch for a while. I tried to no avail to picture the person's face in the balls at the playground. It could've been any face—any face with a Dodgers hat perched on it. I set the alarm for 3am and dozed off around ten.

I'd never claimed to be a good dreamer. Most of my dreams were scattered and unorganized—utterly forgettable encounters with fragments of my childhood or a neutered pish-posh of that day's events. They were dreams with water parks in supermarkets or vice versa, dreams with talking pelicans standing in as my grandparents.

That night I dreamt of a place called the Moose House. The setting was haphazard and aligned itself with the ridiculous mixed-place feel of my usual nocturnal rubbish. It was set in Florida, though a "Florida" with steep cliffs—one of which on top of sat the Moose House. The most surprising thing about the Moose House, to me in my dream, was that it was indeed of house full of moose. There were several of them draped on the front porch just underneath a neon sign that proclaimed the title of their residence. I walked inside and was silently greeted by several more. They were sitting around a big semicircular couch, maybe somewhere between five and ten of them in all, playing some game with dice—dice that were, in retrospect, actually pine cones. A picture of the USS Monitor, the famous Civil War ironclad that duked it out with that other famous ironclad, the Merrimac, clung to the wall behind them. I recalled being surprised at what good listeners the moose turned out to be. I was babbling to them about Kyle and Catbirddog and Dover and the fortune cookie and everything else. They sat there listening without bombarding me with obligatory nods or interrupting me with skeptical inquiries.

Only one moose ever spoke and when he spoke he spoke a lot:

"Let me tell you something about Kyle, friend. You see, Kyle is God. Or he *was* God. He was the all-knowing thing relegated to a sheet of static. He had once long ago been the omnipresent expanse of unmitigated being. Indeed he had been everywhere and knew everything. His sole error was that he gave us choice, and with that choice we chose not to believe. And many of us that did choose to believe really did not but we hoped. Hope and belief are not fraternal. They aren't even flat mates. Hope has allegiance with desperation. Optimism, you say? If you optimistic you are confident. If you are pessimistic you are hopeful. There was nothing optimistic about hoping there was a God. It was based in fear and hope and desperation. Could Kyle rebound? Would new belief give him back his power? Doubtful. Kyle didn't even believe anymore. But he had not been rendered a nihilist. Kyle had an agenda. And that agenda was, of course, destroying the Earth. He wanted to eliminate this nest of non-believers and start all over again. This was once something he could do on his own accord, any day of the week. The Great Flood, remember? Noah's Ark and all that? But now he needs the help of mankind to destroy mankind. He needed Dallas Austin Houston, the only man with the appropriate balance of power and nihilism. But Houston's dead now. Felled by the Cyclical Night, a fraternity of men and women who believed, and they did really believe, that mankind could will itself into Kyle's old territory: that of omnipotence, omniscience, and omnipresence. They were off to a good start. You, Mr. Badger, Kyle had not seen coming. Here's a guy stupid enough to believe the truth. At least, before you sicked that pooch bomb on Houston and then shot like a neutrino through the earth's crust. That's the real problem with you: you really are a true immortal. Not just someone who lives a long time, like those knuckleheads at the Cyclical Night—or Uncertain Stars, as they like to call themselves now. You can't die. Not even if you want to. In the severest breed of unlikelihood, let's say, the monkey on a typewriter who types the collected works of James Michener in chronological order and then encores with *Gargantua and Pantagruel*, you had been born consisting entirely of star dust. And not just any star dust. You're composed of the old Sun of the old Earth: Skyfell 1.0. You're made from the same matter as Kyle, and only one other entity: Dover Datsun. And that's why the two of you hit it off, why the degree of mutual care was so superciliously hefty considering your limited interactions.

"Now why is Uncertain Stars after you? Testing. You're the first true immortal. 100% shrapnel proof. Tether Pass and his gang could not survive an inch-range bomb like you did. They are really, really old, but they are not immortal.

They are susceptible to death. And they are dying: Paulo and Deanwood? Both crunched by an errant blimp—the thing fell out of the sky with gaudy indiscretion and flattened Deanwood's Buick. But Tether and his gang are okay with that. Because they are optimistic. Because they are confident. Because they have Trant's money and power to sculpt their aspirations. And because Whipple has the other one. Whipple has your buddy Dover Datsun, you see?"

The moose lit a Parliament Light Menthol and offered me one. I declined and sat there thinking about what the moose had just told me. The scene shifted about. Moose came and went.

Eventually I asked my moose, "Who landed me the gig at the Stratoport? I have loose memories of it being some kind of witness protection program, but that's about it. I remember being in a white room, filling out paperwork. There were lots of people standing around. And a man...A man in a white sweater, wearing a Los Angeles Dodgers hat. This man, he wasn't young, but he had this smooth white skin, like he'd never encountered the sun or the weather..."

The moose took a drag from his menthol and exhaled. "Benny Briggs."

"Who?"

"The man. His name is Benny Briggs."

My synapses went into action but came up empty. "Who is he?"

"Well, for all purposes, I guess you could say he's the Devil."

"The Devil?"

"Pretty much." The moose had drool oozing out the side of his mouth. He chortled and motioned at the TV, where the Washington Nationals were playing catch and warming up.

"Nats and Twins tonight," the moose said. "Should be a good one. At least 'til the Nats dip into that jerk-off bullpen of theirs."

I woke up and immediately spotted a problem with what the moose had said. The Nationals did not play the AL Central this year hence they would not be playing the Twins. This solidified my belief that taking advice from a moose, dreamt or otherwise, was a dodgy enterprise. But what of the Dodgers hat connection? The face in the playground and this Benny Briggs the moose was talking about? Premonition? Or just residue from a wayward subconscious coming back around on me? Both were legitimate possibilities these days.

I checked the time. It was fifteen of 3am. The TV was still on. Werder Bremen was playing Bayern Munich. The match was only 15 minutes in and Bayern Munich was already up 2-0. The match was a replay, however, and I knew Werder Bremen ends up winning 3-2. A miniature feeling of tragedy: observing the euphoric confidence of a commanding yet ill-fated squad as you watch and wait for them to fudge the whole thing up.

I had been woken by a noise, this much I understood. Ah, yes: the cat. There he is bouncing around with dime-size, nighttime pupils, chasing shadows, jerking his head around keeping track of invisible prey, pausing intermittently to lick his legs ferociously. I lowered my hand and made a scraping sound on the floor, the classic cat lure that no kitty can resist. He regarded my hand briefly before carrying on with his spooky after-hours cat business. Cats got like this in the deep night: mega-predatory, whimsically playful, solipsistic, trippy, freaking people out with that bizarre animal hyperawareness. He seemed to be watching something on the ceiling, blinking his eyes with exaggeration, spazzing his head ever so often as if to get a better view of whatever it was, like you do at a crowded concert with people standing in front of you. Some people think cats are watching spirits or angels or demons when they do this. I always liked to think they were watching slivers of light or floating dust that we humans can't see. I felt myself getting a little spooked so I allowed my mind to wander to cat bloopers. Maybe the funniest thing in the world: cat bloopers. I thought of specific ones I'd seen on television or online: kitties attacking tiny toddlers and making them fall down, kitties getting chased by parakeets, falling off the tops of recliners while sleeping, severely *un*feline-like miscalculations that had them jumping off things and landing in toilets or full bathtubs. The corny ones even cracked me up: kitties on surfboards or wearing aviator sunglasses or yawing and making people sounds. I'd take cat bloopers over the *Three Stooges* any day of the week.

I made a kissy sound and scratched at the floor again in another attempt to get his attention. He regarded me with the same empirical anti-interest.

Then my cat did something that I did not like:

He whipped around to face the door to my balcony and froze in place with his fur on end. Then he hissed really loudly and bounded out of the room.

~5~

The Boy Who Could Fly

Patrick Orville Ulysses Tyrell "Pout" Spivey was born in 1872 on a sinking nameless barge in the Red River. His mother, Sarah Spivey, had gutted the inside of a watermelon and placed the little Spivey inside of it, along with a note of his date of birth, heritage, and name (due to her hurried hand, no one will ever be for sure if the young Spivey's last of four names was Tyrone or Tyrell). She then sealed it with the nautical knots that she knew so well and set him adrift to float at the mercy of the river. A bit of good fortune landed the young Spivey at a bank along the property of a wealthy and perpetually drunk Scotsman named Charlie Parse. Poor Sarah's body was never found.

Mr. Parse was dynamiting gar and shooting at their floating corpses with his pistol when he saw a peculiar vessel come to a stop in the shallow of his bank. He walked over to it, poked it, and kicked it back out to the flow of the river, then steadied his aim and took a few shots at it, missing it repeatedly and grumbling at the tiny taunting splashes of his wayward bullets. Refusing to be eluded by a melon and opting for a theatrical approach to foil his nemesis, he went for his dynamite, lit up a stick and slung it at the melon, plugging his ears with anticipated satisfaction.

The water burped mightily and the melon was no more. He turned around, clapped his hands, let out a syllable hoot and began to pace back to his shooter's mound when a high pitched wail from above demanded his attention. He turned toward the river and looked straight up in the sky to see what appeared to be a bald monkey flying right toward him. Charlie Parse was not a superstitious man. He'd even long ago abandoned the Catholicism that his family and countrymen brought ashore with them, but looking into the gaping mouth of that fierce and flying devil of miniature, that nugget of certain doom, that wriggling apocalyptic side-show, he quickly remembered the name of the one he once worshipped:

"Sweet Jesus! Save me from this cursed daemon, from this bald little flying misery!" he hollered as he balled himself up, his hands around his head.

A soft thump followed by a baby's wail accompanied the quivering Parse on the desolate stretch of bank. Mr. Parse unraveled and rolled over on his belly to face the tiny Hell spawn. He uncovered his eyes one by one and sat looking at the young Spivey until his fear gave way to perplexity. He stood up, brushed himself off and went to fetch himself another bottle and his young wife from inside his manor.

"Woman?"

"Yes, Charlie," she called from upstairs.

"Do yeh like beybies?"

"Yes, Charlie."

"Well, I gawt yeh one. "

"Okay, Charlie. "

"Merry Christmas, woman."

"It's June, Charlie."

Bethany Parse raised little Spivey as if he were her own. At the age of one, he could engage in monosyllabic conversations with ease. His favorite topics were the moon, the sun, the earth, and the sky which he called 'Big Blue." At age two he was zooming through his ABCs and beginning on simple math. One day, at the age of three, while playing outside their manor in the dry dirt among the tiny funneled traps of ant-lions, little Spivey surprised the still very young Bethany by taking a small stick and scribbling a peculiar shape in the dirt, the jagged inches of its edges suggested topography, although it couldn't have possibly been inspired by the atlas in the house which was seldom used apart for supporting the occasional game of craps.

There, sitting in the dirt, he goosed his neck straight up at his mom and said with his monotone pip-squeak voice, "Mommy, this is the place I have to go one day. Can you find it for me?"

Bethany had never expressed an interest in topography, geography, or any other subject that fell beyond tending to her constantly inebriated husband; however her curiosity was quick to blossom when spurred by the young Spivey's tight-lipped seriousness when inquiring about this enigmatic and oblong new development there in the dirt.

"I know I can't go there now, mommy, but I need to know where it is so I can go when they ask me to."

"Who, honey? When who asks you to?"

"The star people."

"And who are the star people, Pout?"

"They're my friends. They're scientists."

"Ooh, scientists."

"Yes, mommy."

"What kind of scientists, honey?"

"All kinds."

"Scientists, wow! Did they teach you about the *din-o-saurs*?"

"Nah, they're not much into paleontology, mommy."

"Oh."

The little Spivey scratched his head and dabbed at the shaped on the ground with his stick, "So you don't know where this is, mommy?"

"No, Pout, I don't believe I do. Is it a state? It doesn't look like any state. Maybe it's a *country.*"

"I don't know. Does daddy know about science?"

"No, I'm afraid that your daddy doesn't know much about any sort of science outside the science of drinking whiskey."

The little Spivey shook his itty bitty head in disappointment and softly patted the palm of his left hand with his stick.

"You should learn more science, mommy."

"I will, honey. Just for you, so I can tell you all about it."

"Will you also help me practice flying, mommy?"

"Practice flying?"

"Yes, ma'am. The star people told me that I needed to start practicing flying."

"They did, did they?"

"Yes, ma'am."

"How you plan on doing that? By jumping out of trees?"

"Yes, ma'am."

"Listen, young man, you will not jump out of any trees! If I even see you climbing a tree, I'll take a switch and tear your little booty up, you understand?"

"Yes, ma'am."

The young Spivey grew to be a strong and lean teenager who divided his time with excursions into the woodland to hunt, fish, and build forts over the Louisiana marshland and trips to Shreveport where he'd sit in the library for hours and hours, soaking up books of all sorts with a consistent interest in topography and history.

One day, among those old musty books, he was visited by strange man, a gruff looking man of fifty or so, who was covered head to toe in a variety of clothes that Pout had never seen before. Tether Pass sat across from the young Spivey and propped his feet up on the desk, ushering trim looks of disapproval from the few other people in the room.

"Doubt you remember me."

"Excuse me, sir?"

"You're the Spivey boy, right?"

"Yes, sir, I am."

"Nevermind the formality. You practice flying like I told you? I hope to hell you did, because the time has come, junior. I need you to fly for me right now, in about ten minutes. Can you do that for me?"

"Fly?"

"Yeah, fly. Like a bird or an airplane."

"A what?"

"Forget it. Look. Here's a hundred dollars. You just follow me and what I tell you to do and it's yours."

Pout picked up the money and looked at it. "This says it was printed in 1988, sir. That's a hundred years from now."

"Let me see…Shit, I didn't think about that. Forget about it, it's just a typo."

"A what?"

"Nothing, nevermind. Christ. How 'bout some tobacco? You like tobacco? Or I can give you some gold. How 'bout some gold and some tobacco, that better?"

Tether offered Pout his Rolex and a pack of Parliament Lights.

"This is some peculiar looking tobacco, sir. Is it from Detroit or somethin'?"

"Detroit? It's from Virginia, knucklehead, where all the other tobacco comes from," Tether Pass said. "So we got a deal?"

"Well…"

"Ah, save it, chief. Follow me. We can shake on it while we're speed-walkin'."

The young Pout shut his book, remembering to himself that he was on page 42. "I'm sorry, sir, but I can't. I mean, you must understand this is all very, very discombobulatin'. I mean, first of all, I can't fly."

"You can fly and you will fly—and you'll be doing your flying in about ten minutes." Tether pulled his slicker back, revealing a duo of Colts 45's.

"Well, I reckon I don't have much choice in the matter. Can I still have the tobacco?"

"It's yours. The Rolex, too."

"The what?"

"Christ, what fucking year is this? The watch. This thing. The *gold*. Take it."

"Oh, okay. Thanks!"

Tether Pass led the young Pout out of the library and into a neighboring field. What appeared to be a giant pine cone, maybe twelve feet tall and eight feet wide, was the only disruption in the green field's expanse. A number of dirty faces in the periphery watched them as they walked up to pine cone. As they approached it, Pout could see the giant pine cone was actually constructed out of some glistening metal that was copper in color. Tether Pass pointed a small rectangular device at the metalloid pine cone and a door opened on its side. They entered the pine cone which turned out to be some kind of vessel. The walls of the craft were covered with graphs and dials and maps and screens and buttons. Tether Pass took a seat behind an oversized steering wheel in the center of it and instructed Pout to take one of three seats against the wall.

"Buckle up."

"What?"

"Put that belt over you and put the metal parts together until they make a clicking sound."

"Okay."

Tether Pass pressed some buttons on console beneath the steering wheel. The craft began to whir and tilt. Pout put his hands over his ears and closed his eyes and stayed that way until the machine came to a rest in Rock Creek Park, a leech-shaped swath of hilly greenery that bisected modern day Washington, DC.

~6~

The Boy Who Could Fly (Part 2)

I stared at my balcony door for a long minute. I felt the cold fire of alarm all throughout my nervous system. The closed blinds offered no information. I saw no movement on the other side of them. I turned the television off. I stood up and went into my closet. What would my weapon of choice be? Eel-skin cowboy boot or Black & Decker Dustbuster? Neither. Croquet mallet—the burgundy one. I recalled what I had rehearsed in my head if a situation like this came about, if I ever had a home intruder. I would not be passive or tentative but instead assault the intruder with an offense of unmitigated unfamiliarity. I'd shriek like a madman, stomp my foot on the ground, clap spastically, bark like a dog, yell all sorts of random insane things at the top of my voice. I even though of which words would work best: Brigade! Sandstorm! Torpedo! I'd go way outside the realm of their experience and make them think *Shit, this motherfucker's **way** crazier than I am!* But I couldn't do any of that. Instead I stood frozen in the middle of the studio apartment, listening.

Two knocks on the balcony door. Soft knocks, like from a mistress's knuckles.

I discreetly unlocked the door—

—and then I pushed it open as hard as I could. I heard the dull thump of object on flesh, followed by an "Ow!" … I held the croquet mallet up. I was about to tomahawk my intruder when a thin voice said, "Please, sir…Don't hurt me!"

A gangly boy of sixteen or so stood there in front of me. His eyes were closed and his demeanor was that of a rookie punter. His outfit was one part Dickens, two parts Dust Bowl. He was wearing a giant cushiony hat, lavender in color, and he had a pistol with a comically long barrel in his hand. He looked terrified.

"What are you doing up here?"

"I think I'm supposed to shoot you with this," he said, holding up the pistol so I could see it.

"Well, you'd better not," I said. "How'd you get up here?"

"You wouldn't believe it. I *flew!*"

"You're right, I wouldn't believe that. And neither will the cops."

"The what?"

"The cops."

"The...cops?"

"Yeah, the cops. The fuzz, the police. You know, John Law."

"Who?"

"What's wrong with you? What's your deal? And why are you here?"

"This fellow gave me a bunch of gold and tobacco to fly up here and shoot you with this thing."

"What fellow? Shit, nevermind, I know what fellow. Where's this fellow at?"

"Down there." The young man pointed at a fellow far below talking at what I knew to be a long lifeless telephone booth.

"Give me that," I said. He handed me his gun without protest. It had no chamber at all and it weighed very little.

"What kind of gun is this?"

"I don't know. He said it won't kill you. He said it'll only put you to sleep."

A dart gun, probably. No doubt loaded with darts soaked in frog poison or sheep's urine or whatever it was they used to knock people out.

"Tell you what. You like gold and tobacco?"

"Yes, sir."

"What else do you like?"

The boy adjusted his vest and tie. Comfort began to seep into him. "Books. I read lots of 'em. Mostly science books. I'm real learned for my age."

The combination of the boy's newfound comfort and nascent confidence blasted me with indignation so I said, "Let me ask you something. If I push you over the side there, do you think you could fly back down to the ground?"

"Yes, sir. But you don't have to push me. I was gettin' ready to fly back down anyway. That is, if you'll let me."

There was something was all wrong about this kid. He was like no one I'd ever encountered before: his speech, his dress, his demeanor. He looked and sounded like he was performing in a play.

"Where are you from?"

"Caddo Parish."

"Louisiana?"

"Yes, sir."

I held up the dart gun/pistol. "I can't believe you were going to shoot me with this. What if you'd hit me in the eye?"

"Sir, I don't want to shoot anybody with anything anywhere. I just want to go back to the library and finish up the book I was readin'…. Can I ask you something, sir? Where am I? I mean I just don't understand this place. Everything is just so *unusual* lookin' and so modern lookin'… I'm in Detroit, ain't I?"

"*Detroit?*"

The boy's eyes froze—they froze on the television behind me. I turned around. Werder Bremen was up 3-2 in the 88th minute. The boy walked past me and up to my TV. He kneeled down and ran his hand across the screen. He poked at it. He tilted his head and looked at it. He stood up and tried to look at it from behind. I did not have a very impressive TV. It was circa '93 and weighed as much as a Waverunner. The boy continued inspecting it. It was like a scene out of the director's cut of *Encino Man*.

He turned to me, his eyes aglow like he had just unwrapped a box full of spotted puppies.

"What *is* it?"

"What's what? The TV? It's a Radio Shack," I said. "Thing's probably twice your age."

The boy looked at me with zero comprehension. His face twitched with a debut of neediness and anxiety.

"I *have* to have one. I have to have a Radio Shack."

"Hell, you can have that one. Twenty bucks, it's yours."

"Twenty bucks?"

"Yep. Twenty bucks."

The boy's face sunk. He looked overcome by impossibility.

"You alright?" I asked him.

"Yes, sir. It's just… That's an awful lot of deer, sir."

"What? Oh, I get it. Twenty bucks, a lot of *deer*. Hahaha."

"Do you want 'em all at once?"

"Do I want what all at once? The twenty dollars? Preferably, yes."

"Twenty *dollars*?"

"Yes. Twenty dollars. What did you think I said?"

"But I don't keep that kind of money on me, sir."

The boy looked increasingly distraught.

"Tell you what," I said. "I keep this gun. You give me that hat. The TV is yours. All that sound good to you?"

The boy glowed with tethered giddiness. He tightened the slack on his gaiety before it overcame him and said, "Yes, sir, that all sounds plenty good to me."

Tether Pass didn't like what he was seeing. He didn't like what he was doing either. That is, he didn't enjoy gesticulating at random and miming the word "rhubarb" over and over in order to feign conversation in a clearly derelict telephone booth, some time capsule from the 20th century (in accord with the circumstances, Tether didn't like what he was smelling either). No, he wasn't enjoying any bit of this. The young Spivey was supposed to fly up to Badger's balcony, shoot Badger with the dart gun, and then unlock his front door. Simple stuff—even for a teenager from the late 19th century. But what was Spivey doing now? He was flying back down—or rather, sort of floating back down. Had Ed Wood concocted this scene, you'd be able to see the wires. And maybe the TV would've been a little bigger—perhaps a little more "Cold War." That's right: the *TV*. The young Spivey was grappling with a TV as he made his descent.

Pout Spivey touched down clumsily but safely. He sat the TV down and then sat on top of it; his timid grin worked its way across the ground and eventually found the eyes of Tether Pass, who was already contemplating depositing him at Dien Bien Phu circa '54.

~7~

The Thing on the Television

Since I no longer owned a TV, I cabbed it over to a 24 hour diner in Georgetown at 3am. The interior of the place was part Polynesian airport lobby, part interrogation room. Everything was either wood grain or flowery. There were two TVs: a big one in the back and a little one snookered in the corner up front. I sat by the little one, against the window. A few Ethiopians were lounging around the bar. Half-a-dozen cops sat around a big round table. They had a seemingly contrived multiculturalism to them, like the cast of Star Trek Voyager or any post-1990 commercial or billboard. Their radios beeped and crackled and hissed while they sipped coffee and muttered to one another.

I ordered a coffee, a plain waffle, and a side of fries, and then I read my fortune for probably the tenth time, examining each letter for some new nugget of information. *Your solar soul mate can be found in familiar dimensions. 4am, channel 208.* Solar soul mate? Dover, for sure. Dover, whom I barely knew, whom I barely remembered. I told my waiter that my cousin was making a cameo on channel 208 at 4am. Could he keep the little TV on 208? No problem, no problem. Channel 208 turned out to be some Christian network. Everything was smiley and clappy; a caricature of a gospel service.

I looked out the window. My thoughts went out of bounds. Actually they went out of bounds and up in the bleachers. Who was the mysterious man in the Dodger's hat? Was his name really Benny Briggs? Do I have any business trusting a dreamt moose? How will the Nationals do next year? What would I have named the Nationals when they moved from Montreal? The Ex-Expos? Would the world essentially be the same if the Dodgers had remained the Trolley Dodgers? Or one of their many other previous names? Would the people of Los Angeles county still root for the Superbas? Or the Robins? Or the Bridegrooms? Was Tommy Lasorda still alive? Had Brezhnev ever watched a baseball game?

It began to rain. And then it began to storm. Thunderstorm. First the flash, then the thunder. These things made sense to me. Thunder always made me hum *Riders on the Storm* by the Doors. Invariably. No regard for circumstances. I was at the "brain squirming like a toad" part when my waiter dropped off about my waffle and fries and refilled my coffee. Everything yellow and brown. Everything except the ketchup. I ate half my food. On the TV: fat people clapping and singing. Minutes crawled by... My waiter was outside smoking. His umbrella was yellow. *He was yellow.*...Bela texted me *(U up?)*, but I did not text her back....What had my life become? It was like a Celine novel: all question marks and exclamation points. It was once a life of squeaky bikes and breakfast with girls in big sunglasses, a life of 5pm Chardonnay, foggy ambles, Scandinavian jazz in my headphones, crossword puzzles, Erik Satie, 7-11 coffee, Midday trips to modern art museums, baseball games... In short, it was kind of neat and kind of normal. And now? Absurd. Utterly nutso.

3:58...

Things changing on the TV: A stage. Entering from stage left: a man in a white suit with a block of white hair with politician's part in it. He stopped and the middle of the stage. He waved and bowed at a seemingly endless sea of heads. The man was craftily illuminated; he appeared to be glowing. He said something and smiled. His teeth were supernaturally white. He started up with the anointed bit: stern brow, mild acrobatics…He sheathed his microphone in his starched armpit and began to clap in rhythm—it was a spastic number that loosened his hair… The stage behind him darkened; a spotlight blasted him. He closed his eyes—and began to sing. This went on for a while. It reminded me of a Russian variety show…

Then a fusillade of Amens and Hallelujahs… Until the spotlight abandoned him for larger prey:

Dover.

But it wasn't Dover. Something was off with her frame, with her shoulders. They were all different. They were swimmer's shoulders: wide with a balled bulge at their ends. And this Dover had not short blond hair but long dark brown hair. The face was at once the same but different. It lacked the tumultuous beauty of the Dover I briefly knew. It was dry of the contrasting emotions that I had seen battle across her smooth symmetry. This woman looked like Dover, but it wasn't her. It was the Dover that my unconscious mind might conjure up in a dream—everything fundamentally accurate and yet impossibly inaccurate. Dover was laughing and pointing at the man. He laughed and pointed back… I needed volume on the TV. Where was my waiter? The TV was too high up, totally remote control dependant. On the TV, the lighting changed. Everything red; violet at the edges. Dover was speaking to the audience. And then everything changed: a look on her face of marauding surprise, a look of ambush. The man in white looked confused. Then he did what he did best: he smiled. Dover ran off the stage, the man clapped, the camera zoomed over a thousand heads, all covered with maxed grins amidst hands in motion. Here and now: the sustained illumination of quick-sputter lightening. I braced for heavy thunder, but it rocked me before its cue and strafed my nervous system. On the TV: the man in white, pacing and talking to his shoes. And on the bottom left of the screen was a ten digit phone number.

I dialed the number…

Hello, and thank you for calling Whipple Van Ward Ministries. To make a donation, press 1. To be Saved, press 2. To talk to a representative, press 3. To repeat these options, press 4.

I pressed 3 and immediately my right ear was assaulted by some hymnal on-hold music:

I was sinking deep in sin,
Far from a peaceful shore,
Very deeply stained within,
Sinking to rise no more,
But the Master of the sea,
Heard my despairing cry,
From the waters lifted me,
Now safe am I.
Love lifted me! Love lifted me!
When nothing else could help,
Love lifted….

click

"Praise the Lord and thank you for holding. This is Jessica speaking, how can I help you?"

"Hey! Couple of questions… First, what is this I'm watching?"

"You are watching the Whipple Van Ward Show," said Jessica she said with a neutered optimism. "Is this the first time you have joined us?"

"Yes, it is. Who was that lady? The brunette that ran off the stage?"

"Let's see, that was tonight's guest who is… Hmm, hold just a moment please."

click

…..my despairing cry,
From the waters lifted me,

Now safe am…

click

"That was tonight's guest who is La Estrella Primera. She is the world's leading….."

"—Who?"

"La Estrella Primera," Jessica said, pronouncing the "estrella" like a true blooded gringo.

"You sure her name isn't Dover Datsun?"

"It just says La Estrella Primera here," she said flatly.

"Yeah, but that's not her name. It doesn't say her real name anywhere?"

"Let me see… No sir, it only says La Estrella Primera."

"Where are you located?"

"I'm afraid I can't say?"

"What do you mean you can't say?"

"Pastor Protocol suggests we don't reveal the location of our base of telephones operations…"

"No, no, not you. I mean the dude with the silver hair. Whipple Van Whatever…"

"Whipple Van Ward?"

"Yes. The gentleman on TV. Where is *he* located?"

"Well, his Outreach program is based in San Antonio—"

"San Antonio? Christ, don't tell me San Antonio…"

"—but his Ministry and Base of Financial Operations are based in Denver."

"So where is he now?"

"Denver."

"That's Denver there I'm seeing on TV?"

"Yes, sir."

I asked for the address of Whipple Van Ward's church/amphitheatre and thanked Jessica and hung up. Van Ward was on the TV talking about the temptation of Satan which quickly segued to pornography on the internet. His forehead was beaded with sweat. A commercial came on about erectile dysfunction, showing a man and woman playing miniature golf. The man's ball, no doubt blue, threaded the blades of a miniature windmill and popped in the hole: a hole in one. The woman didn't fare as well as her little pink ball bounced off one of the blades and into a pond. A tragically animated mallard was there to barrage her with angry quacks...

Just one pill and you can achieve vertical commitment for up to three hours!

.....They hopped in go-carts and began to race around the track, the man, all smiles, zoomed in front of a freckled youngster while the woman waved the dust from her face.

The waiter came by and refilled my coffee and asked me if my cousin was on yet. No, no, not yet, not yet...

I called the number on the screen again.

"Hey! Listen, I just called a minute ago... Is this Jennifer? No, wait, not Jennifer... Jessica! Is this Jessica?"

"This is Dave. How can I help you, sir?"

"Well, I was wondering how I would go about meeting Mr. Van Ward in person. I'm a big supporter, and a big booster, and I just realized I've never actually met Mr. Van Ward and I just want to shake his hand and thank him for all that he's done for me. Is this kind of thing possible?"

"It is, but it's the Lord Jesus you should be thanking, sir. Mr. Van Ward is just—"

"I don't want to thank Jesus. I want to thank Mr. Van Ward."

"Okay, sir, I can help you with that. What I can do is I can give you the number for the Outreach Ambassador of First Encounters Relations and they can sign you up for an Encounter with Mr. Van Ward."

"Super duper." Dave gave me the number and I called it.

"Praise the Lord and thank you for calling Outreach First Encounters

Relations. This is Wanda, how can I help you?"

"Hi, I'd like to meet with Mr. Van Ward. I'm one of his biggest fans."

"Okay, sir, we can arrange that. Would you like your Encounter to be in Dallas, Denver, Houston, Phoenix, or San Antonio?"

"Denver, please. That's where he is now, right?"

"Yes sir, I believe he is in Denver. When would you like to have your Encounter?"

What was up with this "Encounter" business? "As soon as possible," I said. "How about the day after tomorrow."

"The day after tomorrow…That would be the fifth. Yes sir, we can arrange that. Let me notify you that there is an additional fee for an Expeditionary Encounter."

"An additional fee? What's the non-additional fee?"

"You mean the fee?"

"Yes."

"It's $333 for an Encounter, and the expeditionary fee is $100."

"Yikes. That's a pretty steep handshake."

"Yes, but you understand 100% of the fee goes to Mr. Van Ward's Base of Financial Operations…"

"I bet it does."

"What's that, sir?"

Nothing, it's nothing. I gave Wanda my information and cabbed it home and booked a flight to Denver for the following day. I fell asleep wondering what Colorado's nickname was.

~8~

Unexpected Halos

The first thing you notice when you exit the Denver airport is the horizon. It proclaims: let there be no mistake, you are now in the West. The second thing you notice is a gigantic statue of a bright blue bronco with fierce red eyes. The thing is reared up on it hind legs, its front legs pawing at the air. It is either spooked or furious. Satan's Stallion, Mustang from Hell… I knew Denver's denizens did not approve of their unlikely mascot, however I was quite partial to it. I found it to be an oblique testament to opportunity. Welcome to Colorado, it seemed to say, where even the horrible likes of me can exist. And of course the third thing you notice is that 17% decrease in oxygen. Your first bout of physical exertion is followed by a mild dreamy collapse. You take to lite beer and spontaneous naps and all your dreams take place underwater.

The bus from the airport was crowded. I discreetly observed the other passengers. Different breed of folks out here in the West. The overall size of your average human increased about 15%, and the mustaches are without irony.

The bus deposited me in a derelict part of downtown. I went into a taco shop and had a burrito and a coffee. I acquainted myself with my map while I ate. Then I walked around downtown for a little while. Beware of the grid in Denver. At some point it swaps on you: North/South becomes Northwest/Southeast. Just keep track of where the sun is and you'll be alright.

My hotel was easy to find—it was the only business on the block still open. The lobby had been glossed with a layer of late 21st century Bohemia—the scruffy, flannelled concierge, the Built to Spill that petered out of a boom box, the seemingly newly-applied purple paint on the walls, the wannabe-IKEA furniture, the overall flagrant dismissal of color coordination and theme—but it did little to overcome the joint's core personality: Mold, atrophy, dereliction, filth. The fifteen bucks a room all but solidified it.

My room was cold and squeaky. The floor protested every footstep. *What are you doing, man?* it seemed to say. *You know what could happen if you keep doing that?*

The hallway was wide and sort of doubled as a community room. There were a couple of desks, a few couches. A banged-up little TV was camped out under an honest-to-God portrait of Madame Chiang Kai-Shek. The other tenants were sparse and exclusively male. They floated around in shorts and flip-flops and white tank-tops like they were on house arrest. All of them were bald. They sat and smoked and scribbled in notebooks. They drank juice and hot tea and went for long prodigious pees. They reminded me of cuttlefish and body snatchers. I don't think any of them had a laptop or a cell phone. I briefly talked to one of them about the weather. It was a short conversation, half the length of his cigarette. The man and I never breached query and fact but it took an hour for the queasy sensation in my stomach to subside.

It was 7pm on a Tuesday but it could've been any time. I was to meet this Whipple Van Ward at 10am in the morning. My plan was to extract the whereabouts of Dover Datsun from him. I was certain it had been her on the TV. She had changed, for sure, but it had been her. Where was Tether Pass? Would he be following me? His operation had seen better days it seemed.

I asked the concierge about bars. I cabbed it over to some joint in another neighborhood. The place was named after a popular bus line. Pictures of Elway were all over the walls—sometimes stereotypes come through for you. I ordered a Maker's Mark neat and a glass of soda water. The stereo played good Classic Rock: Hendrix's *Axis: Bold as Love*, McCartney's *Band on the Run*, some early Yes…The crowd was a crowd that could have been from any metropolitan area in the United States. Primarily a bunch in their twenties and thirties, all of them with customized trigger-happy laughter and declarative statements that curled up at the end like questions, tangled up in conversations about International Development and cities in India or Central America…All of them vaguely despicable. I watched a baseball game with the bartender. Dodgers at Rockies. Colorado was the Centennial State: such an arbitrary nickname. Why not the Mountain State? Everything else here was

Mountain this and Mountain that…Where was the man in the Dodger's hat, this Benny Briggs fellow that my inner moose had told me about? My inner moose?!

At that time I didn't know who Pal Iberville was—so it was no surprise that I did not recognize him when he sat down at the barstool next to me. I did, however, realize something was up when Led Zeppelin's *Fool in the Rain* was followed by the first track on Astor Piazzola's *Rough Night and the Cyclical Dancer*, a difficult segue no matter what kind of DJ you are. Other people noticed the transition too, most notably the bartender, who went off somewhere to inspect what was going on with the stereo.

"You keep track of these guys?" Pal asked me, indicating the Colorado Rockies. He was a miasma of Polo Crest.

"Not really, but I understand they're not doing too well."

"Certainly not in this game they aren't," Pal said. The Dodgers were up 12-3 in the bottom of the ninth.

"For sure, for sure," I said. "Although being a Nationals fan I'm kind of prohibited from discussing the woes of other baseball teams."

"Nationals fan? You from Washington?"

I laughed. "Who ever heard of a Nationals fan that wasn't from Washington?"

"Good point."

I had switched to beer: some microbrew that tasted like fermented pine sap. Piazzola was replaced by the Marshall Tucker Band. The bartender reemerged and Pal Iberville ordered a pint of Fat Tire. The place was filling up. I was getting tired.

"Are you from around here?" I asked Pal Iberville.

"No, I'm originally from South Louisiana," Pal said. "Cajun Country."

"Good food down there."

"Good everything down there except weather."

I paid my tab and shook Pal's hand. We mutually declined from introducing ourselves and I was okay with that. I would have had trouble summoning up a decent fake name. Little did I know it didn't matter what name I fed him anyway.

I stood up, put on my scarf and coat. On all the televisions: waterfalls and springs and geysers. Odd commercial: advertising what? Ah, yes: overactive bladders. My own bladder asserted itself and I went to the men's room. The door was locked so I waited. I waited a while. I tried the door again. I waited some more. The door clicked, unlocked itself. I opened it. No one was there. The sink was left running. There was steam on the mirror and an arrow drawn in it, an arrow pointing to the Dodgers hat that was hanging just to the left of it. I took the hat. My size: 8 ¼. A tag hung from it, a tag that said:

Put me on and keep your dukes up

The mysterious Benny Briggs strikes again. My reaction was that of dull surprise. Christ, I'd become jaded. I put on the hat, took a twenty second piss, and walked back out. A few more patrons were at the bar. Only two seats were now empty: Mine and Pal's. I went outside. The city's glow didn't squelch the endless swath of stars. Stars made me think of the Stratoport, where I became intimate with stars on a nightly basis. I wondered how Bentley and Ms. Maps were doing. The closest thing to suicide: total disappearance, which is what I'd achieved, as far as the two of them were concerned. I briefly basked in mild forlornness until it gave way for my concern for their concern (if they were indeed concerned). Then all this concern of mine got locked up in dreary practicalities, like being concerned where the hell I was…

They say the kneecap is the most painful place to get whacked. That's probably because nobody's whacked them in the kidneys yet. I never heard or saw my assailant, but I sure as hell smelled him: Polo Crest, maybe ten spritzes worth.

"*Stop*," was all I could manage to say. "*Stop*."

Would Pal have stopped? I guess he had to at some point, but that point wasn't anywhere on the horizon. Pal spared my face but laid into my ribs and stomach and kidneys and everything else below my Adam's apple.

I remember the Jurassic wail of big brakes applied with fierce impromptu. I remember the smell of carbon monoxide, straight out of the exhaust pipe. I remember a bus—a blue and white bus—and then the sound of many feet on pavement and a low grumble of muttered malice. My new mantra abandoned my mouth and moved elsewhere. *Stop* had applied itself to the lips of my assailant. *Stop, stop, stop*: over and over and over…I watched Pal get swallowed up by a small gulf of blue and white. I couldn't see him but I could hear him. And then I didn't hear him anymore…Eventually he reappeared but he was upside down. And he was a different color. Pal was now red. Crimson red. I remember thinking: Mussolini's body: this is the same thing they did to Mussolini's body…

"You okay, man?" Another Dodgers hat. A face beneath it. Young, black, sweaty.

"Yeah," I said, lying. "I'm alright."

"We saw that son of a bitch jump you. So we pulled over and jumped *him*."

I leaned up. Dodger's fans. Dozens of them. Some standing there looking at me, some getting back on the bus. All ages, all colors, both genders.

"Thanks," I said, with the appropriate apprehension of volume and syllables.

The young man put my newly acquired Dodgers hat back on my head and helped me stand up…More pain. A good pain: a pain from conflict, albeit the one-sided variety.

"You sure you're okay, brother? You need a lift somewhere?"

The man was squatting. I shook my head. *No.* He seemed a little peeved, disappointed. Others approached… I declined everything I could for the next ten minutes….

Transit again: the Denver Light Rail. I looked out the window at the lifeless streets and then I examined the round effeminate letters that sprawled across my hand conspiring to create some strange, esoteric message: *Something and Osage or Osage and Something!!!*

A lot of ding-ding-ding, this light rail. My car was empty, save the driver: a milky fellow, hairless and expansive. Was he good at trivia? Could he name the biggest city in the world named after a person?

"This is you," he said.

This is what? "This is what?"

"You. This is *you*. Osage Street."

I hopped off the light rail and walked in the direction of what had to be Venus.

"Tether here."

~muffled sound, vague panting~

"Somebody karate chop your esophagus, bud?"

~whimpering, more panting~

"Oh, bud, I bet you haven't picked a single rose for me, much less a blue one."

~weird howl, more panting~

"Hey, bud, how about you try me back when you ain't got so much bubbly gum in your mouth?"

Thresher is to bedlam what Great White is to whatever it was that had eaten up my Wednesday morning. While I was dreaming a peculiar dream about playing a game of baseball in some Pixar rainforest, the Reverend Whipple Van Ward managed to pull off a very thorough Brezhnev. His helicopter exploded all over some cherubic suburb south of Denver in the slim hours of the morning and he had the misfortune of being on the thing. He was flying his plastic surgeon back to the Colorado Springs. No investigation yet but authorities were already stringing together words like "drone" and "hacked" and "kamikaze" and "assassination."

I was watching TV coverage in the community room of my hotel and I was raising my voice for the first time in years. A cluster of the same strange, cephalopodan tenants were giving me some grief about the TV's volume.

"What's *with* you guys?" I said to them.

"It's supposed to be muted all hours."

"I need to see this. I need to *hear* this. I had a meeting with this man today."

"Put the subtitles on."

One of them coughed and another one said, "Bless you."

"Why the hell did you bless him? He didn't sneeze, he coughed!"

"Mute it or I'll go get the proprietor."

"*You* mute it." I looked at the four of them. They were lounging around like they were pantomiming a scene in a hot tub. Their demeanor was obnoxiously sedate. "What's *with* you guys?"

"What do you mean what's with us? What's with you?"

I didn't fare much better at breakfast. I went to a little diner a few blocks over. Old antlers were all over the walls, and every critter that didn't boast an exoskeleton seemed to have come here to get mounted. More taxidermy than Clark Gable or Hemingway ever could've built up.

My scrambled eggs had a little flag in them, a flag with a design I recognized: George Washington's coat-of-arms, more commonly known as the flag of the District of Columbia. DC's flag. And in-between the two bars were two words in all caps: *HURRY HOME!!!!*

No thanks to that. No, I don't think I will hurry home. So sorry, Mr. Benny Briggs or the Devil or whoever you are. Or should I hurry home? Two favors he's done me already by way of his little messages. Why shouldn't I go along with this one? Simple, because a good-sized chunk of me felt this one was different, that it was delivered by someone else. If not the Devil then who? God? God would probably use all caps like that before anyone else would…And four exclamation points? Any cursory examination of the Old Testament would indicate that He might be prone to exaggeration or overemphasis. Christ, I'd forgotten though: God meant Kyle. Or Pass and his gang. Or Dover and me. God was up in the air, so to speak. Any number of men or women might be God.

So who the hell was responsible for the message in my eggs?

"I can literally see your wheels turning," said the man in the white sweater and Dodgers hat. Benny Briggs, or the Devil, or whoever he was took a seat at my table.

"I'll change my name to Mary Grace if you're not Benny Briggs."

We held eye contact. The man wasn't albino, but he sure as hell didn't have a drop of melanin in him. His face was featureless: no facial hair, normal nose and lips, dull eyebrows, uninspiring blue eyes. He was like the actor you throw opposite a lousy lead to wring out the latter's attributes.

"You may keep your name, Mr. Badger. I am indeed Benny Briggs," he said. "I mean, that's one of my names. I have a damn reservoir of them. In fact people call me all kinds of things. Satan, Lucifer, Beelzebub, the Devil…"

I leaned back, broke eye contact. "You know, that was some pretty grody usage of the word 'literally'."

Benny Briggs smiled. "The supreme pet peeve in the English-speaking world is improper usage of the word 'literally' and as you can surely imagine, I have to manifest evil any and every way I can. This provides me with more than ample opportunity. You'd be surprised how upset people get when I'm *literally* a basket case, or I *literally* kick the shit out of someone, or I—"

"—literally see stars?"

"Yes, or *literally* run off with my tail between my legs—which I suppose I have actually literally done before."

"This your flag?" I asked, tapping the little flag.

"No, that is not my flag." Briggs plucked the flag from my eggs and examined it. "It appears the Devil has a copycat."

Briggs became pensive. He softly put his index on my fork as if he were checking its pulse. The fork blurred and where only a second ago was a fork now sat a magnifying glass.

"How'd you do that?"

"The Devil has embraced nanotechnology," he said with a taught grin. He then examined the flag with the magnifying glass for some time. His demeanor grew worrisome for both of us. "Ah, Christ. I knew he'd be coming around sooner or later…"

"You knew *who* would be coming around?"

"Who do you think?—the friggin' anti-Christ."

"Really?"

He smirked and shook his head and for the first time the Devil looked like the asshole that everyone made him out to be. "No, not really. This, friend, is the handwriting of your buddy Mr. Catbirddog. I hope somebody's told him that cacti aren't indigenous to Colorado."

The waitress came by and deposited a glass of ice water in front of Briggs. Briggs gave it back to her and requested a glass of water without ice—a tiny display of evil, as far as I was concerned.

I scratched my head and looked out the window. No cacti, just newspaper machines and skinny, shriveled up trees. "Why does Catbirddog want me to go back to DC?" I asked.

"Because he's a bounty hunter, and Weldon Trant and the syrupy leftovers of the Fraternal Assembly of Texas Trillionaires have offered a very large sum of money for Dover Datsun. Catbirddog probably doesn't want you anywhere near Datsun. To him you're just an additional element to this equation. Simplify, simplify: works for all sorts of vocations and ways of life—even bounty hunting."

"How big is the bounty on Dover?"

"Why do you want to know?" Briggs asked with contrived suspicion.

"I'm just curious."

I watched Briggs while he got symmetrical with his napkin, fork, and knife. I noticed his upper lip had the mild vertical wrinklage of a middle-aged French woman, and his skin was the kind of dry that a single Dasani could probably fix up.

"Three million dollars," he said.

"Wowsers, that's a lot of money."

"Not for Trant and his buddies."

"Do you know where Dover is?"

"Of course, I do," Briggs said. "I, too, am omniscient. At least, mostly omniscient."

"Mostly omniscient? That's an oxymoron if I've ever heard one."

"I knew you were going to say that."

"So why haven't you nabbed Dover and collected the bounty yourself?"

"Because I don't care about any bounty. I don't like money. Money and I just never got along. Money and I are sort of like competitors—we both claim to be the root of all evil. No, I don't like money at all. Nor do I need it. Being the Devil, as you can imagine, gets you all sorts of perks."

I took a bite of my room temperature scrambled eggs. My bacon was limp and fatty. My toast was saturated in butter.

"Evil breakfast here, that's for damn sure. Want some bacon?"

"Devil's a vegetarian."

"Figures."

Fire trucks went by. Lots of them. The sirens squelched the restaurant's Muzak.

"Would you tell me where Dover is?" I asked the Devil.

Briggs leaned back and stared at the ceiling. "Put yourself in my shoes for a minute," he said. "What would be the most evil thing to do here?"

The fire trucks kept coming. Big fire somewhere. False alarms have a transparency to them that disallows the sort of zealous flurry that was whirring by my window.

I adopted a gravid demeanor that seemed to suit the occasion and said: "The most evil thing to do here is to tell me where she is."

~9~

Decimal City

I stopped by some sort of enhanced convenience store. Opera boomed out over its entrance in effort to keep the loitering down. I bought a five-dollar pen, some graph paper, and a bottle of Cutty Sark with a handle on it and went back to my room. I got pretty lit and then organized a plan. I made a bunch of phone calls. I tip-toed down the hall to get some ginger ale to mix with my booze. Cutty Sark: a whisky named after a boat named after a poem. I fell asleep with my clothes on and the overhead light on and didn't wake up until the sun blasted me in the face—that Denver sun means business.

8am. I checked my phone's history to make sure I'd really made all those calls and hadn't just dreamt it.

A lot of people champion the Bible as the most beneficial book they've ever read. Not me. Not right now, anyway. Mine was *Donkeys Can't Sleep in Bathtubs and Other Crazy Laws*, written by the otherwise anonymous Susan Dach. Good book; essentially a collection of those absurd blue laws that got penciled in in county seat courthouses all across America when she was still figuring out who she was. Weird laws like: it's illegal to bring your lucky rabbit's foot to a barbershop in Clayton, Alabama; or: it's illegal to wear a cactus suit on Wednesdays in Denver, Colorado.

The initial misdemeanor charge turned Hyde real quick when Catbirddog decided he didn't want to be handcuffed. They had to taze the old boy six times before they could get him inside a squad car. A few of those cops got pricked pretty bad, granted I felt no sorrier for them than I did for Catbirddog.

I took the light-rail way out the dull and dusty hum of Denver's fringe. I took a bus to that took me to another bus that took me to Decimal City, Colorado, home of La Estrella Primera, also known as Dover Datsun.

I got off the bus in prairieland. The stop reminded me of the scene in *North by Northwest* where Cary Grant is attacked by a biplane. Where would I hide if a biplane attacked me? No cornfields around here, just the jagged immensity of the Rockies in the distance. A bland fear balled up in me. I surveyed the sky for biplanes. There were no biplanes—but the sky was not empty. A bona-fide zeppelin floated high directly above me—a silver dirigible straight out of 1920's Berlin. The big thing was lumbering westward, its implied purr buried in the breeze. I watched it for a while. I had the feeling it was watching me. The sun hit it right and it momentarily became illuminated. A convoy of military vehicles with jungle camouflage went snarling by. I crossed the street and hopped a fence, following my memorized directions to Dover Datsun's house, occasionally looking back at the now distant zeppelin.

I was walking in what seemed to be the middle of an enormous Technicolor green field. I counted a total of five trees—all of them decidedly Tim Burton and seemingly not wanting anything to do with each other. A duo of silhouettes loomed on the horizon—that of a silo and a large house—Dover's house.

The sun had disappeared behind the Rockies by the time I knocked on the door. Bats and chimney sweeps zigzagged around the silo. A trio of haggard sunflowers swayed like drunks at the foot of the porch. Coyotes chirped in the distance.

The "Dover" that opened the door was the one from television, although the yard-range proximity endowed me with the knowledge that this Dover, however dissimilar from the one that buzzed around the entrails of my memory, was indeed the real Dover Datsun.

She wore a light grey sweater over jeans; she was staring at me with an empirical curiosity. Did she even recognize me?

"I thought you were dead," she said.

"What made you think that?"

"National Public Radio."

"They have that in Texas?"

"They do. They also have it in the Yucatan," she said. "So you're not really a suicide bomber?"

"If I am, I'm obviously a pretty lousy one."

This sort of aloof bandying went on until my brain started to hurt more than my feet. I invited myself in. Her carpet was thick and her couches were plush. The brittle boned could thrive here for years without an ounce of worriment. Modernist piano and incense that smelled like Catholic Mass did well to push the surreal factor into plain ol' weird.

"Nice place."

Dover came over and sat on the armrest of the couch. "There's a lake out back, a little one."

"A pond, then."

"No, too big to be a pond."

"Swimming and fishing allowed?"

"I suppose so, though I don't know what you'd fish with, and I don't know what you'd fish for. You can swim all you want, though, provided you're okay with freezing to death."

I tugged at invisible hair. "Brunette."

"Sometimes." Dover took off her hair, her wig. Her real hair was blonde and very short, maybe three weeks past a boot camp buzz job.

"I keep it short now. Do you like it?"

"I do like it," I said. "Plus it goes with the music."

She held up the wig, maybe pondering it, maybe thinking about something else.

"How long have you been here?" I asked her.

"Years and years. Five years. Off and on. I have a place in the city, in Denver. I come out here when I need to get away."

"Get away from what?"

She shook her head. Okay, sure, she doesn't want to talk about it right now, no problem.

"Are you hungry? Do you want anything to drink?"

I asked for some water. I was tired. Dover brought me a bottle of Evian and I took a big vertical swig of it. Then I took off my shoes and lay down. Within two minutes, my mind swerved over into bumpy terrain of my subconscious. Oh, no: Sleep? Right now? Yup...

I woke up lying in bed, fully clothed underneath several layers of sheets and blankets. I was surrounded by a small phalanx of multicolored throw pillows. Sparse sunlight snuck through the cracks in the Venetian blinds.

Where the fuck was I?

I lay vacant of thought for a solid minute until I was able to make sense out of the clock on the wall:

7:25

Okay, sure. AM or PM? I had no idea. I began to have some success replaying the events of the previous day. My head felt numb, my body spent. There was seemingly no end to the bed I was in. I covered my face with one of the pillows and moaned.

I found myself in a state of limbo, my eyelids played screen for interactive dreams. I ran through a town of tall windmills, looking for Dover among the townsfolk. They all knew her but didn't seem to know where she was. I came to a dense market situated under a bridge where men with grey skin were swapping fish, all sorts of fishes and shellfish. One man was carrying a huge sailfish, yelling at the people in front of him to get out of the way in some language I'd never heard before. Dover was there, cutting her way through the crowd on a tiny scooter. She was beeping at everyone and handing out little leaflets. She smiled and gave me one. On it in a glitzy font read the word "adhere" over and over.

Adhere adhere adhere adhere....

Adhere to what?

An ambitious wind descended. Cash from the fishmongers' booths fluttered in magnitude. There was a big scramble, people everywhere snatching money out of the air and off the ground. Dover disappeared in the pandemonium...

The sound of light footsteps gliding down the hallway pulled me away from my limbo. I got up and tip-toed to a bathroom. I pissed the length of a prime-time commercial break and splashed my face with cold water. I found some Pepsodent in the medicine cabinet and brushed my teeth with my finger.

I walked down the hallway. I was upstairs. I went down the stairs, stepping over a big fluffy cat who had taken up residence in the middle of them. The smell of coffee pulled me to the kitchen. Dover was sitting at the dining room table, in her robe, doing a crossword puzzle; a newspaper was scattered in front of her.

"Good morning, sunshine," she said. "Sleep okay?"

"Yes, I did. I slept very well."

"I'm making us an assortment of muffins. Coffee?"

I accepted and poured myself a cup. "How did I...?"

"Get upstairs?"

"Yes."

"I walked you up around midnight."

"I don't remember that at all. I must've been out of it." I took a sip of a deliciously adequate cup of coffee and said: "That bed is the most comfortable bed in the universe."

"It is, I know."

"It's a very difficult bed to get out of. A black hole bed."

"I agree 100%. I spend the first hour of every day mired in it."

"What about today?"

She set her pen down and took a sip of coffee. Her short hair was wet and matted to her head.

"I was good today," she said. "I jumped up and took a shower before I could nod back off."

"But you slept...?"

"In my bed, next to you."

A desperate sounding buzzer raised hell in the kitchen: the muffins are definitely ready, it proclaimed. Dover went to the kitchen to retrieve them and for the first time I realized the stereo was on: PM saxophone and brushy drums slid across the carpet, up my leg, and into my ears—at least, that's how I envisioned it happening.

Dover came back with a large tray of muffins. She ran me through the different flavors: lemon, chocolate, honey nut, raspberry, blueberry, of course...I played muffin roulette and took one at random. I took a committal bite. Lemon. The tiniest of catastrophes.

Dover said, "You're a sleeptalker."

"What do you mean?"

"You talk in your sleep."

"I do? I did? What did I say?"

"I couldn't understand you. It wasn't English you were speaking, it was something else."

"Bizarre."

"How many languages do you speak?"

"One and a half."

"The half?"

"Kitchen Spanish."

Dover pondered this. We contentedly sipped our coffees in silence. The blinds were closed. I was thirsty.

"No, it wasn't any kind of Spanish," she said. "It sounded Eastern European."

I shrugged. *Forget about it.*

I poured myself a glass of water and topped off my coffee. Tiny rumbles in my pocket: my cell phone, vibrating. One new message:

Morning, 4. TP here. Practice your baffled face. The cows are coming home at 9am sharp.

My psychological makeup grimaced and persevered, like a maimed grunt. I needed a shower. I wanted a shower: the thirty-minute variety. Two bathrooms: a gigantic one and a large one. I used the latter, which was downstairs. Dover instructed me to use the red towel and the blue washcloth, then she recommitted to her crossword puzzle. I took my slow, languid shower to the escort of tangible daydreams.

I dried off and dressed. Dover's chair was empty. The ceiling creaked. I went upstairs.

She was in her room, on her bed, 100% sans clothing. She was sitting up, Indian style, with a crossword puzzle on a huge hardcover atlas. "The secret to my lack of success," she said, referring to the puzzle. And then:

"What was Pike's first name?"

"Pike?"

"Yeah," she said. "*Pike's Peak* Pike."

"Oh. Zebulon."

"How do you spell it?"

"Z-E-B-U-L-O-N."

The bed was made. I hadn't made it. Dover said: "There's no protocol. I don't get guests. It's all foggy all the time. This is weird?"

My standards for what was weird were stratospheric and I told her as much.

"What's that vowelly game with the real hard ball?"

"Jai Alai."

"Spell it."

I spelled it and then she said: "Would you rather fill me up or make me sticky?"

Okay, now things were getting weird, granted in a positive sort of way. Regardless, I was done responding. I walked over to the window and peaked through the blinds. It was 8:30am. I turned back around and looked at Dover. My libido cowered. Some atavistic nugget in my noodle had apparently suggested this was not the time or place to try to reproduce.

3's there with the first of the herd. They're on the perimeter of the house, lined up from noon to 3. Noon being north. You inside with the target?

"My favorite thing about this place is..."

Affirmative. Where? I don't see 3 or herd.

"...time doesn't defeat you. Time does what I want it to do here. It serves me. See, look... It's tomorrow already."

I went downstairs and got more coffee. Sax and drums had been replaced by an ambitious flute. The coffee was burnt and cold so I loaded it up with cream and nuked it. I went into the living room and turned the TV on and watched it fizz for a little while. *3's there with the first of the herd.* I was told I would recognize 3.

I went back upstairs and asked Dover if she still wrote Haikus.

"No, not anymore. Well, every now and then—but on accident."

"Who are you now, Dover?"

She stared into space; her pupils unloosened and surveyed the wall as if searching for a mosquito.

"I don't know," she began. "I really don't anymore. I've outgrown myself. I occupy too much space. That's why I come here: to whither. I come here to whither back to normal. They post everything on me. Heinous things and also things that are good. But it's all still things. It makes weight and I'm small. They thrust their image onto me; they try to transform me into the person they think I am. Or they subtract from me. They chisel at me like I'm the Berlin Wall or something. They break off pieces and take them home. I'm all over the place. Parts of me are everywhere. I feel like a mutant compromise, some horrible pastiche. So I come here to cut myself off from them, to kill off the infected parts of me and let myself regenerate among my fresh carrot juice and '80's music."

"Who chisels you? Who adds to you?"

"My followers. They gobble up my identity—or they jettison my identity. I'm all over the place, in bellies or up in the sky. I don't know who I am anymore, so I come here."

"Do you want clothes on?"

She ignored me and continued: "Identity is so nebulous. It's a gaseous thing, not a thing for fences or cages. It's like a cloud of ash from an Icelandic volcano. You know it's there. You can point at it and say 'hey, that's a cloud of ash,' but when you get up in it, it changes on you. People's identities seep in and out of each other. It's an unconditional interchange with all sorts of results. It's a jumbled mess. How did we ever do it? How did we ever keep who we are? How did I keep who I was? Everett, it's so complicated for me, which is why I come here. My biggest dilemma here? Which soap to use: the aloe/ginger/salmon roe rub or the aquatic mammal bone marrow blend with maple and hickory? My dilemmas here are good dilemmas. My dilemmas out there are not good dilemmas. I come here for the preferable dilemmas."

I nodded. No argument here. How could there be? I excused myself and went to the restroom. It had been a while since someone had called me Everett. It felt good. I looked out the bathroom window. No cows and no mysterious 3 either.

Are you sure 3 is at the right location?

Has to be. No other house inside ten miles.

Confirm for me?

Roger that. Will do.

"Who was the Soviet Union's head honcho in the '70s?"

She was on her belly now, her legs jutting into the air like searchlights out of Vonnegut.

"Ha," I said. "B-R-E-Z-H-N-E-V."

"How do you pronounce it?"

I pronounced it and said, "Your new dilemmas… I don't mean any offense by this, but what makes you think people care enough about you in the first place to want to take the time to persecute you? And who are these followers you're talking about? Are you some sort of celebrity or something? What is it you do now, Dover?"

She held eye contact with me. I sat on the bed so she didn't strain her neck peering up at me. I feared that I offended her.

"I predict stigmata," she said. "I am in the business of predicting stigmata. It's a very tricky task, and you have to be exact, otherwise…"

"How do you predict stigmata?"

"I use premonitions. And drugs. Over the counter drugs. Once a week, right before I go to bed, I take six tablespoons of NyQuil, eight high-potency B-12 tablets, four phosphatidylcholine pills, three heavy-duty multivitamins, half a rophenol, two Sudafed PMs, some Advil, a glass of Tahitian Noni juice, and a shot of whiskey. The effect is an array of Technicolor dreams, and about once every six months a stigmata will occur in one of these dreams, usually in some dusty shanty full of people with cardboard skin. It's easy. I just ask someone in my dream where I am and what day it is and, voila!—stigmata predicted."

"Then what?"

"Then I tell my press agent and the third world goes nutso."

Incredible. Did I know anyone with a normal job these days? I asked her, "Have you ever been inaccurate?"

"Absolutely. Several times. Oh, it's awful. The demographic I deal with are desperate, ignorant, and overwhelmed with anxiety. When I let them down, they are absolutely grief-stricken. And then they are furious. A dud leads to calls for my head on a platter—literally! It's stressful, Everett. It's like an ICBM of stress. I have been called the Virgin Mary and I have been called the Antichrist. God, it's all destroying my complexion."

I touched her face. "No, it's not. Your skin is super smooth. You don't have a single blemish."

"Thousand dollar makeup."

I ran my finger along her lips. She winced. *Tickles.*

Outside a dog began barking. "You have a dog?"

Different kind of wince. "No."

I shifted my position and lay down next to her, propping myself up with my elbow. Dover stood up. It was probably coincidence but indignation still seeped into the room like poisonous gas.

"Where are you going?"

"To get my robe."

"Why?"

"To go outside."

"What for?"

"To see what's tripping my alarm."

To fall asleep I pretend I'm in the Sargasso Sea. Not the real deal, with its implied stratus of seaweed and its unhurried wind, streaked with clinical vessels full of chipper, bearded ecologists, but the Sargasso Sea from the florid lore of the Age of Sail, with its Pudong of battered masts, its undulating favelas of half-sunk clippers and freighters and humbled wartime pedigree, huddled next to each other in preposterous angles, or frozen in disgraceful mount. Nobody sees the sun in my Sargasso Sea. The bunched-up hours of light are simply cessations of darkness. There is an unseen menace in the sky. A dragon, maybe, or a sentient flying machine. It is somewhere above me, searching. I am in a tiny raft, nestled amongst the decay-veined behemoths. I have hidden myself as well as I could using only an old shred of tarp and small but undeterminable number of life jackets. I lay motionless in an abstruse position to squelch my humanness, to blur any familiar outlines or angles that my predator might recognize. And then I fall asleep...

Air-raid sirens and distant tornadoes aside, few sounds are more ominous than that of an approaching helicopter. It was the sound of a helicopter *receding*, though, that brained me that blurry morning in Dover's house...

I stayed there two days before everything thoroughly sank in. I watched Bonanza and played with the cat and read a book about the Barbary Coast (Dover had boasted a dubious book collection: the contents of her shelves were primarily composed of bubbly travel journals with names like *Peeling Tamarinds in Bucharest*, or *Untangling Shoelaces in Ouagadougou*). I checked my bank account online and didn't blink for ten or fifteen seconds. I began trying to construct what I'd tell the authorities, who would most assuredly come by to investigate why I had been rendered a millionaire by way of a single midnight transaction, a *heritage mysterieux* from a source laden with coy acronyms.

I had stayed inside that morning, as instructed, and peeked through the blinds.

Cows are what I saw: lots of them, lined up in formation, their posture rigid with false biology; their eyes aglow with malignant sentience. And I saw Javelin Till, wearing parachute pants and an XS cardigan, and pointing something dark and metalloid at Dover.

I couldn't see the chopper until it landed. It looked like a military arachnid, the product of some punk rock branch of Skunk Works. The thing's windows were tinted, but I knew who was inside of it. Then something happened: something like an altercation between Javelin and Dover, followed by latter's acquiescence with her queer new predicament. I watched Dover Datsun as she stepped up and disappeared into the opaque thorax of that evil-looking machine.

I didn't see her again for nearly 150 years.

Epilogue:

Skyfell's Remainder and the Sea of Shapes

2156. The future is every bit the manic, heavily-tentacled monster made of eyes that everyone thought it would be. The element of the 21st century had been fire; this century's element is water.

Revelation, the Book of Daniel: they never happened—but they might as well have. Plentitude and options reign supreme. All is attainable and hence undesired. There are primarily two states of mind: deep apathy and insanity, and little lies between them. Information has thinned to transparency. The internet convulsed and wriggled until it finally worked its way into humanity. We now know everything and hence very little at all.

The bombs and missiles never came. The idea of war, never mind the actual practice of it, became so thoroughly exhausting that we actually abandoned it. Sloth triumphed over aggression. Entertainment did away with religion-fueled hatred and every other reason to start throwing rocks. It was all but confirmed when we sicked the nanos on the world's uranium, neutering the 50,000 bombs while they lay in their subterranean slumber. Something like a new Cold War did develop between us and the Chinese. They threatened to all jump at once, prompting us and the rest of the West to do the same: the idea being to knock the world off its axis, therefore pretty much ruining the party for everybody. The Big Jump never happened, though. Mother Earth neither wanted nor needed an assisted suicide—she could do it all by herself. The fires started up and then they didn't stop. At least, not until the water intervened. The island nations were the first big casualties. The two Koreas finally embraced as they drowned; the Vietnamese took to boats for the final time, as did the Filipinos and Indonesians and Pacific Islanders. London and Tokyo built their big bubbles, keeping out the water, but holding in and nurturing the neuroses that eventually imploded them.

DC has changed a lot. The skyline shot up like fast-forward sunflowers around the middle of the century, right about when hoverboards finally hit the market. Then the water happened, so now the city quivers above a brand new sea on hectares and kilometers of stilts and springs. Ambitious little DC, for so long snookered between Maryland and Virginia, became a titanium colossus of interchange, nourished by the chronic lightening and endless brigade of skeletal windmills that spin dizzily in its shadow.

I'm pushing 190 but you wouldn't know it. My physical make-up hit a plateau somewhere around 50 and I've made the most of it. My build is still deceivingly academic, regardless of how many push-ups and sit-ups I do or don't do. My bones and muscles and tendons and ligaments and organs and systems all still continue about their business unabated. I guess. I hope. No docs, just an android dentist that speaks Turkish as a first language: My body is simply don't ask, don't tell. No atrophy up top either. My mind buzzes with information, and I've got eleven anecdotes for every possible set of circumstances, domestic or otherwise, you could ever come up with, yet a benign jadedness keeps my ego muzzled and mutes any desire to remark on every pleasure or displeasure, no matter how appropriate or correct—you err exponentially less when you're 190 and you goddamn well know it. All this, I know, renders me very *attractive*, and I've taken maximum advantage of it. I never did marry; consequently I probably lapped Wilt Chamberlain before my centennial birthday. Love's dried up. My rendition of it is a sort of enhanced fondness, tethered by eminent ephemerality, meaning the death of whoever I'm hugging or kissing or fucking, regardless of how grand or puny their stature. Whatever I have is to be eventually lost. I have proof, and the notion is despotic and shows no promise of capsizing. Friends are chosen carefully and infrequently. Adults and kids are interchangeable in 2156: the latter are often steeped in the news, which is essentially a cluster bomb of numbers and letters spewed out of the mouths of a thousand talking heads, or pornography, which abandoned standards long ago and is now an erratic cornucopia of flesh and sound and liquid, while the adults, whacked out on bubbly optimism, mumble things like: "Would you rather eat poo or boogers or both?"

My life? The folks within it? The ones I told you about are all gone, presumably for good now. Catbirddog escaped from his little cell there in Denver and worked his way south to hide among his prickly brethren. His zipper got stuck and he got posthumous revenge on the world at large when a trio of teenage Mexicans tried to gut him for agave. Javelin Till, or 3, married Pal Iberville in Massachusetts and they adopted a little Indonesian boy named Flak who they rechristened Sherman Panzer Iberville-Till. They ran a Go-Cart track outside of Jasper, Indiana until the fields gave way to new rivers. The Passes and I actually became friends. We played paintball and card games until they went off to Mars, along with just about every other sucker who'd ever seen *Total Recall*. The Dodgers won every pennant from 2020 to 2036 until someone somewhere, out of mangled desperation, sicked an honest-to-God platoon of priests, along with their arsenal of holy water and crucifixes, on the franchise and their mysterious owner, one Benjamin Briggs, who eventually sold the team after they were relegated to being the doormat of the NL West for the ten subsequent seasons. The devil indeed went down to Georgia, though, where he bought the Atlanta Braves, who have since won eight World Series in nine attempts (the lone failure a four game sweep by the Los Angeles Angels). Kyle I never saw or heard from again. I did, however, one day happen upon a peculiar piece in the City Paper's *News of the Weird* column about a man arrested at a Best Buy in Tallahassee, Florida for attacking a flatscreen TV because the thing had allegedly whispered to him over and over: *please kill me please kill me…*

     I was in the Rue Dubai, a showy joint that hung on to DC's underbelly like a glass remora, when she walked in and sat down next to be at the bar and ordered a Wolf Blitzer.

     "Wolf Blitzer?" said the bartender, a slim kid with ambiguous lineage and wearing sky fatigues. His N-FO glowed on the top of his hand: *Wolf Blitzer (the drink): rum and coke in a coffee mug.* He assembled the drink with a gymnastic panache he had not presented when opening and delivering my Kirin Ichiban.

     Dover looked appropriately different. She also appeared as if she was lurking around 50 years old: her hair was still short, only now stylishly gray and sturdily pricked up with wax. Her still athletic body had gathered tiny patches of mass in the usual battle zones. She was wearing a long sea green dress and zero accessories aside from a pair of decidedly Fellini eyeglasses. She had a delightfully superficial air about her, like a gal who, reared on a steady diet of Kierkegaard and Krishnamurti, finally gives way to the perfume samples and trim gossip of *Vogue* and *Cosmo*.

     I turned to her and said: "I'll be damned. This whole time I thought the

Statue of Liberty was up in New York."

It took her about five long seconds to figure out who I was, and then an additional five seconds to figure out I was making fun of her outfit.

"Christ, you again," she said. "You know, I would've never taken you for a tattletale."

"Let there be no mistake, I did it for the money."

"I know you did it for the money. Why else would you do it? Besides, they told me you did it for the money."

"Three million's a decent chunk of change for a perpetual hundredaire like myself," I said. "In truth I did it for us, Dover. You and me. I figure this eternity business will go a hell of a lot smoother if we're loaded."

"Likely story."

"Hey, if you're upset with me, that's not a problem. You can take your half and dangle. No hard feelings on my end."

"My half?"

"With plenty interest, of course," I said. "How's the haiku? You must be a trillion deep in them by now."

"I gave up on them. Nobody reads anymore. Not even haikus."

"No new Bashos on the horizon?"

"No anything on the horizon except the two-toned apocalypse," she said.

"Here you are being poetic and factual in the same breath. You really going to jip posterity and hang up the haiku?"

"What posterity? *We are* posterity."

"Yeah, I guess we are. Posterity in motion," I said. "Cheers… To posterity, obviously."

We clinked our glasses.

The two-toned apocalypse Dover referred to was the light grey/dark grey combo of sky and water. The floor beneath us, like just about everything else in the Rue Dubai, was made of transparent glass. We paused to silently address the shapes in the water beneath us.

On the subject of the *shapes*: When the water came every secret behemoth that ever spawned a thousand tales in the Age of Sail came out to play. We were all okay when it was just new big mammals, with their towers of spout and walls of baleen. It wasn't until the Megalodons showed up that we quickly and thoroughly removed ourselves from the seas. Evolution is an erratic bastard, though, and about as predictable as a winged jellyfish. Preposterously big sharks, it dictated, still conducted their business in the shadow of Darwin like everything else, and it was no surprise that the Megalodon, the caricature of a predator that it is, wound up as prey. And the predator? Humans, of course, if you could still call the queer tribes of industrial diaspora that tore down their houses and factories and civilizations and made haphazard underwater vessels out of them "humans." Nemos, we called them, predictably enough, waging war on the Megalodons in their Quick Subs.

When the shapes receded, I said, "Every piece of cartilage in my body's telling me you don't give a damn about me."

"I can't love you. You know that."

"I do know that."

"It's too…obligatory."

"It is, indeed," I said. "You expect me to expect you to love me out of obligation? Forget it. And I'll tell ya, I'm done with the wooing business."

She moved her seat a little closer to me. "God, it's freaking me out. I can't handle it."

"You can't handle what? Us? This?"

"No," Dover said. "The bartender. He needs a belt. He's a nice guy, and he's got some style going on, but I don't understand why he doesn't wear a belt."

"Maybe he took it off to hang himself. This place always so empty?"

"I mean, his pants…They're not even that tight!"

"I'd offer him mine if it wasn't a collectable."

A loose hour went by. Our drinks got stronger and more accessorized.

"We should stay like this," Dover said.

I watched the grenadine work its way to the bottom of my Bahama Mama and said, "Like what, like drunk?"

"No. Like *this*. Like confidantes. One day it's just going to be us, allegedly. Imagine the two of us completely and thoroughly alone in a world of nothing. We have to be prepared."

"We'll wear white gowns and speak like we're in late Beckett. Quick syllables, everything implied."

I wondered if she had read late Beckett in the 150 odd years since I had seen her.

"If we ever decided to have kids, would they also be immortal?" she asked.

"Not if we adopted them."

The bar casually grew more populated. A guitarist began setting up on a little stage. The musicians of the world in 2156 are not human. They looked and behaved like humans, but were in fact 100% synthetic. Rubbers, we called them, derisively, after their skin, contracted out and supervised by the government, the result of a law passed to deflate the population of human musicians around the turn of the century. Anyone can play guitar. It's true, like they said. Problem is everyone actually started playing guitar—and drums and bass and brass and everything else. Then they took to Eno's creed: Studio as instrument, which quickly sequed to bedroom as studio. Before long the whole world sounded like a five year old being tickled. Noise. All give and no take—no one *to* take, as there were no listeners anymore. The world became music, but it wasn't music (I posture myself as an authority on the matter since I was alive when actual music, the thing you created and practiced and honed, still existed). The fines were slight at first. It wasn't until they killed your electricity for a month that people started dragging all their shit up to the Federal pawn shops.

The thing on stage, which was modeled after a popular singer/songwriter from the early 21st century, complete with the original's strategically mussed mane and arbitrary inkage, had the audacity to put out a tip jar. Then it started up with its pre-show chatter. Synthetic or not, musicians still dosed their audiences with the same dull, haphazard banter every chance they got. Self-deprecating jokes, neutered anecdotes, chockfull of fragments and run-ons…

"How are you, Dover?"

She responded with two negative words that formed a positive phrase: "Not bad." Then she asked how I was.

"Chipper as kipper. Life is swell, and getting better every score or whatever."

"When are you being either profound or facetious?"

"I'll be quiet as a louse if R2 here ever tunes his axe."

She laughed a good deal at that, a cerebral laugh, like it was an inside joke or something. Her breath smelled like booze. Maybe she'd become an alcoholic. Hell, why not?

I stood up and went to the bathroom. I peed and then gargled faucet water. The strong smell of the odorized pucks in the urinal made me nostalgic for something or someone somewhere. Christ, a mirror. My eyes were red and glassy. Two shirt buttons unbuttoned. Make no mistake, mister: you are drunk. A *monologue interieur* began to take shape. Someone came in so I started washing my hands. He peed a good deal and left. Just me again. "She loathes herself," I said aloud to myself. "Can you believe it?" No comment. Apparently I wasn't sure if I believed it. The only evidence I had to go by was a diffidence that had worked its way into her posture and tone of voice. Her wrinkles gave no hint to either an excess of smiles or frowns. In any case, what had I learned about girls that loathed themselves? If you had interest in them, you did not treat them nicely. They will feel they do not deserve it and therefore have no respect for you. A terrible set of circumstances all around. Be mean to the one you want to love. Brezhnev could maybe vouch for this. Fortunately I had no longer had any agenda with Dover, so I felt no compulsion to treat her like shit or otherwise. As I said, love's dried out. Someone else came in to pee so I started washing my hands again. Then I made myself symmetrical and went back to the bar.

We sat in silence for a good while. It was neither the comfortable variety nor tense. The musician was still noodling around on stage. The place was, I estimated, at about half occupancy. Dover had mysteriously switched to beer. She was incessantly picking at the beer bottle's label with her fingernails, peeling little strips off and mangling them between her pointer finger and middle finger—the same way I execute fleas. She lined them up and thumped them off the bar in rapid succession. Someone somewhere once told me that this was a sign of sexual frustration, but then I'd been told lots of peculiar idiosyncrasies were the work of sexual frustration. I was capable of lending the benefit of the doubt to each and every one of them if I needed to.

"Shit."

"What?"

"That."

"What about it?"

"Hurts."

She was referring to the feedback that kept swelling up. The thing on stage was now troubleshooting with the microphone. These things should have roadies or technicians. Maybe that's how I'll make my next three million...

Dover, I could tell, was under the assumption I was still a nice guy. I don't know why, but that unsettled me, made me indignant, but it did, and any slight now would just be pawned off on drunkenness. In short, I was stuck with being nice. Fine, fine...

"What happened to you?" she said.

"What do you mean?"

"When did you become such an asshole?"

I smiled and she frowned. A slim second of summary. Contentment at the expense of another. The alleged musician started playing his first song. It was just him, an acoustic guitar and a little drum machine. The song was good, a hooky number with just the right amount of catharsis. The verses were gritty and followed by a subdued, straightforward chorus that bubbled with inert turbulence. Sublime stuff. In short, I was impressed.

Dover liked it too, for some reason or another. She was enrapt and all her limbs were slightly engaged.

"Dance with me?"

"I'm American, babe. I only dance when I'm taking dancing lessons."

"Pretty please?"

I didn't so much as dance with her as I did stand there and let her dance in front of me. I swayed and wiggled a little bit. 190 goddamn years old and I was still self-conscious about dancing in public. People were looking at us. I pretended not to care. It wasn't hard. Chorus again. Soft and quiet. My little sway was inadvertently appropriate. We leaned into each other. She kind of kissed me and then hugged me so hard I lost my balance.

The thing on stage really did have a voice. I remember the original and I liked him plenty, but his replica maybe surpassed him, granted the circumstances lent it plenty of doubt. I mimed the lyrics as they worked their way up from some basin in my brain...

> *Bellowing a billow of flames*
> *With the fuel from the dance floor*
> *It's for us*
> *—and the cherubs*
> *Proof that we had a ball*
> *We will get what we want tonight*

...Frankly I don't remember if I got what I wanted that night or not.

~~~~~~

It's tomorrow already. Again. In this place that is no place. At the tippest top of Andromeda.

And at the summit of Zillion A.D.

A lifeless cascade of yesteryear's radio waves. Again. The Beatles crackle and fizzle and dissolve into Saturnalian thump. The thing that is me in midst of the middle of it all. Again.

Always/forever.

Old familiarity floats by, swivels, floats back by.

Suspicion has its place even here. It's my cosmos. And I've long forgotten how to share.

Or talk.

To her.

So I wave.

And she understands.

Hello Goodbye.

Made in the USA
Middletown, DE
03 January 2020